NO GETTING OVER YOU

ANNIE DOBBS
EDITH GRACIE

Leighann Dobbs Publishing

This is a work of fiction.

None of it is real. All names, places, and events are products of the author's imagination. Any resemblance to real names, places, or events are purely coincidental, and should not be construed as being real.

NO GETTING OVER YOU

Copyright © 2017

Leighann Dobbs Publishing

All Rights Reserved.

No part of this work may be used or reproduced in any manner, except as allowable under "fair use," without the express written permission of the author.

* * * * * * * * * *

When Katy Wallace left the small town of Vine Falls four years ago, she thought becoming a different person would be everything she ever wanted in life. But when she is offered an opportunity to become the next Mrs. Tipton Van Warner III, she isn't sure living the life of someone else is what she wants anymore.

Uncertain and confused, she goes home to think and runs straight into Matthew Shaw, the one man she probably should avoid. Given the crushing way she had left him, sneaking off without a word the morning after they'd shared the most perfect night ever, Matthew had every right to hate her although four years apart hadn't dimmed her attraction to him in the least -- he still takes her breath away.

Katy has to admit she loves him every bit as much now as the day she'd left Vine Falls...but how could Matthew possibly still love her?

CHAPTER 1

The front door banged shut and Matthew glanced up from his seat in the corner to see which of his friends had decided to come into the Horseshoe early tonight. Fully expecting to see BobbyJoe and LoraLynn, or Sadie, or Amber, or Jensen, he was momentarily stunned when he recognized just who the newcomer was —only she wasn't a newcomer at all, and time seemed to stand still.

Four years ago, she had been a regular. Four years ago, he'd thought she was going to be his wife. But four years ago, Katy Wallace had walked out of his life as casually as she'd just strolled back into the bar where she used to hang out with him and their friends, and time seemed to fall away.

Letting his eyes roam slowly over her, drinking in

the changes four years had made, Matthew noticed that, other than looking a little more grown up, Katy hadn't changed much at all. Her hair was different. Instead of two dark chocolate braids swinging on either side of her face, framing the dark-rimmed glasses she wore, her hair fell in one long, thick rope of a braid down her back to her waist. The long, angled new cut of her bangs curved over her forehead, caressed her cheeks, and ended in a soft spill that ended just below her jawbone.

Silhouetted as her features were, he couldn't see her eyes but he knew if she'd turned to look at him he would find himself drowning in the brilliant cobalt blue of her gaze before her thick lashes swept downward to hide their allure, saving him from a most willing death.

Quietly, he watched as she picked up her drink then reach up to tuck a strand of bang behind her left ear with fingers still as long and delicate as he remembered and he wondered if they would still feel as soft as he remembered them to be, too.

His heart squeezed as memories tripped through his mind like devious wood sprites—something he'd once called Katy. She loved the woods and being out in nature so much he'd dubbed her his own little fairy.

Once upon a time, he'd enjoyed nothing more than watching her frolic among the trees on the riverbank down at Rumor Creek—but that was four years ago and today she didn't look like the type of woman who loved to frolic anymore.

No, he realized with a frown, even the way she moved her hands to tame the wayward bits of her hair was different. Before, she would have made a hasty sweep without thinking. Now the movement was slower. Refined. Far more controlled, and he caught himself wondering if such would be her nature now.

Again, Matthew's memories decided to do vicious things to him by calling up another time, in another place, when he'd scarce dared to catch a breath for fear of becoming suddenly bereft of the feel of her beside him. His brows flew downward and he shifted to resettle himself in his chair.

Katy hadn't seen him yet—at least he didn't think she had. She'd walked in and right up to the bar to order a drink, smiling when the bartender welcomed her back and then asked if she wanted "the usual" for old time's sake but she hadn't once looked his way.

Was that why she was here, why she'd come back to Vine Falls? For old times sake? Something in him wanted to stand up and roar in selfish gratitude but he cautioned the beast to lie still. Katy might be back in her hometown for the first time in four years, but that didn't mean she'd come back to *him*.

Thanking the bartender, she lifted her drink to sip at it through those full, dusky rose lips Matthew remembered so well. By shape and form and petal softness, he knew just how they felt fitted to his own and how they made his breath lock up in his chest when they hovered near his earlobe. He knew how they curved a certain way when she gave him her own self-branded version of a particularly mischievous smile that meant she was up to no good, and how the bottom one tasted, plump and ripe and sweet like the summer plums on the tree down at Rumor Creek when he caught it between his teeth to playfully punish her for her deviltry.

After what seemed like an eternity, she lowered the glass, letting the icy tumbler rest in one palm while she supported it lightly with her other hand and turned to look around the bar. Matthew didn't move.

Hell, if asked later, he'd swear he hadn't dared to breathe in hopes she would not see him there. Not yet. He needed time to adjust, to re-familiarize himself with the idea of her actually being home again.

Utterly still and barely breathing, he waited as her eyes scanned the dance floor and even peered into the adjoining room where the pool tables were, but she didn't appear to have noticed him and he sank down a bit in his chair, relaxed now that he was sure she hadn't seen him there in the shadows, and let his gaze drift, leisurely taking in the rest of her.

She was wearing a white cotton tank top beneath a denim overall dress; he could see how it hugged the curve of her waist before disappearing beneath the blue fabric of her skirt and his fingers itched to slide along those same lines again—for old times sake. Still slim and lithe, from her sun-bronzed shoulders to the slope of her hips and down to her delicate toes, Katy was every bit as sublimely beautiful today as she had been four years ago.

But she was a thing of the past. His past.

Four years ago she had walked out of his life without a word.

He'd bought a ring. Planned to propose the very next day. But morning had been too late.

He'd woke alone. She hadn't even left a note.

She'd run home in the dark, packed a suitcase, and caught the first bus out of Vine Falls before he'd even opened his eyes.

Back then, there had been only one thing in his life that meant anything at all to him—and she'd rolled out of it without even a goodbye, leaving him with nothing but a cold metal band sporting two years worth of hard work in sapphire and diamond and a message with her mother asking him not to follow her; there was no future for the two of them.

Today, she'd breezed back into Vine Falls as if nothing had happened, and as his gaze traversed back up her body to her face, he realized what his friends frequently accused him of was true. For four years, he'd waited, putting his emotions on hold in hopes of a moment just like this.

Dammit.

Four years should have *changed* something, should have made a *difference*, but looking at her now Matthew realized time hadn't done a damn thing to ease the ache where the two of them were concerned. She still looked like every man's dream and he still wanted her. More than that, he still wanted her to want him, too.

She must have felt his gaze because she turned slightly to the right and peered, narrow-eyed, into the shadows surrounding the table where he was sitting. Their eyes locked and Matthew felt the burn of a million bolts of lightning searing him from the inside out, reminding him in an instant of how torn he'd felt the day she'd left him—of the sheer agony of loving her.

Without a word and without relinquishing his visual hold, he got up and headed across the bar. He didn't stop when he reached her, though. He didn't pause at all, not even to say welcome back or offer a simple hello. Instead, he walked right past her and straight out the door to his truck.

After four long, miserable years of secretly hoping she would return, Katy Wallace had finally come home. His entire reason for being was definitely back in Vine Falls, was even now standing right in the middle of what was once their second favorite haunt as a couple—a couple all their friends had believed were destined to be together forever—and he wanted nothing to do with her.

Half an hour later, he was standing in the calf-deep grass at the base of the giant oak on the south bank of Rumor Creek, staring at the spot where they'd spent their last night together.

Unlike today, the grass had been short and soft then; not one blade had pricked their bare feet then, nor her bare skin later through the buffalo checked blanket he'd spread on the ground beneath them. Not a single stem had dared protrude on their day of happiness.

Katy had been endearingly impressed with his showing of a "romantic side" he'd never revealed before; instead of ribbing him for his attention to detail as some of his male friends no doubt would have done, she'd praised his thoughtfulness and marveled over his taste for things both fine and fancy.

She had even given him a particularly memorable kiss in thanks for the surprise he'd had waiting for her on that warm summer afternoon—a candlelit dinner complete with a huge bouquet of roses, cut crystal glasses to drink the chilled wine from, and dual place settings of of the finest china dinnerware from which to dine—all of which he'd secretly filched from his mother's china cabinet. Except for the roses. Those he'd picked from his mother's rosebushes; her pride and joy, second only to her sons.

Matthew had slipped down to Rumor Creek earlier in the day to set everything up—a dinner fit for a woodland fairy princess laid out in the middle of the clearing circled by trees on the banks surrounding her favorite place to swim. And they swam there together that day. Completely in the buff, they'd laughed and splashed and drifted on their backs in the cool water for what had seemed like hours before finally climbing out to dry off and warm themselves with wine and heady kisses that had taken his breath away.

Later, Matthew had lit the candles, laid out the food, and served Katy what he'd thought would be the first dinner of the rest of their lives. More than once that afternoon, he'd put his hands into the pockets of his denim shorts to make sure the ring he'd spent the past two years saving for was still safely in place. He was planning to give it to her that day, but he'd been waiting for that one special moment when he knew the mood was right for him to give it to her ... only that moment never came.

Squeezing his eyes tightly closed in an attempt to block out the pain of memories made more vivid after her reappearance today, Matthew bit back a curse and leaned toward the oak, his clenched fists resting on the rough bark while his torturous thoughts took him back to those few final hours of blinding bliss spent with Katy in his arms.

Like the drink she'd ordered at the bar earlier, Katy had been a virgin. He was her first lover and he remembered being damned proud of the fact that she had allowed no other man to touch her, to love her. To worship her body the way he had that night.

Beneath a canopy of a million twinkling stars, their sun-bronzed bodies bathed in the soft glow of moonlight, they'd made love. After, he'd held her close, her body safely tucked against the curve of his as she'd slept, her pleasure and satisfaction so complete she hadn't been able to hold open her eyes for even a simple goodnight.

Instead, a contented sigh and a kittenish purr of appreciative pleasure had slid softly from her lips as she'd curled into him and fallen asleep while he had lain awake, staring up in happy satisfaction at the stars thinking about how he would wake her in the morning with the ring and ask her to be his bride.

How foolish he had been, believing nothing could touch them in that moment. How foolish he had been to think cruel morning would follow the same rules as did magic midnight. How utterly and completely foolish he had been to trust that Katy had felt the same as he, and that his love would be enough to carry them through. How could he have believed one night would be enough to secure the rest of their lives?

Foolish, foolish, foolish. Matthew thumped his fist against the tree in rhythm with the words, ignoring the bite of the bark and the sting of raw flesh where it dug into his skin, tearing it open under the force of his pummeling. How could he have been so blind?

That night four years ago, he had fallen asleep secure in the belief that morning would go exactly as he'd planned it. Nothing could have prepared him for waking up with empty arms and nothing but cold blankets surrounding him in the place where Katy should have been. No one could have convinced him at the time that she would leave him without a word, a thought, or even a kiss goodbye—and most especially not without explanation—but that had been exactly what she'd done.

Pity had lined her mother's expression that morning when he'd banged on the Wallace's door.

"She's not coming back, Matthew," Katy's mother had offered with a mixture of equal parts patience and sadness when he'd demanded to know where Katy had gone and why.

"She says she doesn't belong here in Vine Falls, that she was meant for more than this, and she doesn't want to be here anymore."

Struck dumb by the fact that his love for her hadn't been enough—that *he* wasn't enough for Katy despite what he'd believed the night before— in that moment, Matthew had shut down, cutting himself off from everything and everyone who could possibly cause him pain. But now the greatest, most excruciating agony of his life was back—and she was already wracking him for her next great torture, as if he hadn't been dealt enough four years ago.

Matthew felt weak, defenseless now in the face of her return, and he hated it almost as much as he'd thought he'd come to hate her. Worse, however, was knowing the truth—that throughout all those years he had been deceived; he'd been lying to himself the entire time.

He still loved her.

Deep in his heart, he knew he would always love Katy, but this time, he thought, he'd be safe from the pain of loving her because *this* time he was prepared. This time he already knew what he should have know all those years before—that she would never love him back.

CHAPTER 2

Heart thumping furiously against her breastbone in an erratic rhythm she hadn't felt in years, Katy Wallace took a slow, deep breath, closed her eyes, then quickly opened them again before trying to walk the twenty or so paces from the bar to a table near the dance floor of the Horseshoe without making an idiot of herself.

Four years abroad had taught her better. Keeping one's cool no matter the situation was one of the first skills Eleanor Van Warner had drummed into her after she'd learned her son had gone and popped the question, asking Katy to marry him after a mere two solid years of casual dating.

She managed, somehow, although her blood was still thrumming through her veins at a rate that had her cheeks burning and her palms ridiculously damp—something that never used to happen to her before she'd left Vine Falls.

Sliding into a chair that gave her full view of the dance floor, the billiards room, and the door—not that she had any particular reason to want to see the door, she told herself—Katy sat her untouched drink on the table and delicately fanned at her cheeks with her hands. The diamond on her left one caught the light, low as it was this early in the afternoon inside Vine Falls' only hot spot, reminding her why watching the door in case Matthew came back was not good, but—*wow*.

Even after four long years, Matthew Shaw was still a heartthrob. He made *her* heart throb anyway, Katy admitted, and a few other places she wouldn't dare mention to anyone—ever. But she knew allowing herself to be affected by him in any way was not a good thing. Breaking out into a sweat of longing the first time she'd seen him again was bad. Watching the door in case he decided to return was even worse. Engaged women did not keep an eye out for ex-boyfriends no matter how hot they were—or how much history they had between them.

"Katy? Katy Wallace, is that you? Oh, my word! You're gorgeous!"

Recognizing the voice as belonging to one of her best friends in high school, Katy turned to confirm it. Grinning, she said, "I have to say the same for you, Amber Lewis. You haven't changed a bit."

Standing for a hug, Katy went through the motions of greeting an old friend before resettling in her chair. She motioned for Amber to join her at the table. "Sit. Let's catch up. What have you been doing for the past four years?"

"Oh, the same old same old," Amber told her, waving away the past time as if it were nothing as she slid into a chair on the opposite side of the table, effectively blocking Katy's view of the door. "You know how it is. But *you*—"

Sitting still while someone's critical gaze analyzed every facet of your appearance and the person behind it made judgments you were uncertain of was a bit unsettling, but Katy did not allow her expression to change until Amber shook her head slowly, and whistled low. "What?"

"Oh, come on. New hair style? Not a stitch on you that isn't from the brands only the glossies know?" Her hand came up and she waved it toward Katy's glasses. "Hell, girl, even your frames are straight out of Snoot Fashion Daily."

Unthinking, Katy lifted a hand to her hair, self-consciously pushing a loose strand of bang behind her ear. "The hair style is sheer self-preservation, actually."

Dropping back in her chair, Amber said, "I don't know where you disappeared to, but if this is how everyone returns, I'll have a ticket, please."

"Thank you—I think," Katy said, taking the backhanded compliment for what it was instead of trying to decide whether or not there was more to it than exactly what was said. She wasn't up north anymore and not everyone said one thing while the intent of their words held an entirely different meaning.

"Forget about me," she said with a wave of her hand, "look at *you*." Katy subtly changed the direction of their conversation to focus on Amber. "You're beaming! I don't think I've ever seen you glowing quite like this. Not since—"

"Since the night Ethan finally let me ride home from school after the game in the front of that big old truck of his?" She grinned and Katy laughed at the memory.

"You had such a thing for him then." Her eyes widened. "Did you—are you and Ethan...? Did anything ever come of that?"

Amber snorted and rolled her eyes. "No, no. Good God, no. Ethan and I were never meant to be—unlike you and Matthew," she said with a wink, and then waved her hand about dismissively. "But this whole glow thing you're seeing might have something to do with how happy I am now that Duke and I finally tied the old knot."

Katy noticed Amber couldn't seem to hold back her grin and her own lips curled in response. Her grin widened. "Doober? You married Doober Noble?"

Amber nodded, looking pleased as punch. "Yep. It only took me a year to decide Ethan wasn't ever going to ask me to do anything besides let him give me a ride home in his truck. Soon as I figured that out, I knew Duke was the one for me."

Katy couldn't stop grinning. "Well it certainly seems so and married life definitely agrees with you. How long have you two been together?"

"Three years this spring."

Katy watched her smile turn wistful as she toyed with the set of rings on her finger, having dropped into a moment of thoughtfulness apparently filled with fond memories. Leaning forward, she patted Amber's hand. "I'm happy for the two of you. Belated congratulations."

"*Very* belated." Amber laughed. "So what about you? Did you finally come to your senses and realize it was time to get home and claim your man before he gets snapped up by some other woman?"

Katy put her hands in her lap, hesitant to show off her own ring. Now just didn't seem like the time, especially when she was still trying to figure out why she'd flown all the way home herself after such a lengthy absence.

During the past four years, she had begun to believe everyone in Vine Falls would have long since forgotten she even existed. But judging from Amber's comments, her friends—some of them, at least—had always believed she would return. Eventually.

To marry Matthew.

Her gaze flew past Amber to the door again but he was not there. She had known he wouldn't be. The way he had looked at her, or rather, looked *through* her on his way out of the Horseshoe earlier was indication enough that *he* certainly wasn't eager to see her again, no matter how the rest of her friends might feel.

Feeling flushed again, she folded her hands in her lap and twisted her legs to the side, hiding her need to move, to fidget, beneath the folds of the checkered tablecloth. "I'm only here for a brief visit, actually. I hope to get to see everyone before I leave again, though, which is why I'm here. Sadie and LoraLynn and the rest of our little clique do still come in here on Friday afternoons, right?"

"Yeah, but usually later," Amber answered. "BobbyJoe's working with Jensen now, so LoraLynn and Sadie usually wait and ride in with them. Of course LoraLynn—wait." She paused, frowning momentarily, and then she arched an eyebrow. "You don't know about that, do you?"

"Obviously not," Katy replied with a tiny smirk.

Again, Amber waved her hands about. "Right, right. Anyway, about LoraLynn. She and BobbyJoe moved into the old Baker place a couple months ago."

Katy's brows rose and Amber nodded.

"Oh, yeah. Put more than a few old noses out of joint, but she never put her chin down, not once." The wry curve of Amber's lips said more about how surprised she'd been than her voice let on. "Told her parents she loved BobbyJoe and they didn't need a piece of paper from anyone to make it okay for her to be with the man she was going to spend the rest of her life with anyway."

"*Our* LoraLynn?" Katy was suddenly dumbfounded. That *was* surprising news. Of them all, LoraLynn was the last person Katy could imagine upsetting the balance in Vine Falls. And with something as big as moving in with her boyfriend? Shacking up, as the elders would have called it, was highly frowned upon and the LoraLynn she knew would never have done anything to make the elder set frown.

Katy, however, was frowning. "What happened, Amber? The LoraLynn I knew was more strait-laced than all our parents put together when it came to marriage coming first in a relationship. Certainly before setting up house together. She must have been terrified BobbyJoe would leave again if she didn't do something drastic..."

"You know a lot about that, too. Up and leaving?" she clarified at Katy's blank stare. "We call it pulling a Katy now. You know, like you did with Matthew?"

Ah, here it was, Katy thought. The moment she would be grilled to within an inch of her life about why she left, and she braced herself for the onslaught of questions.

Amber arched a brow and peered up at Katy, her expression curiously accusing. "You never did say why you left us the way you did. Disappearing overnight without a word—not even a goodbye. What was up with that?"

Katy was saved from having to answer by Duke's arrival. In true whirlwind fashion, he immediately stole Amber's undivided attention, leaving Katy sitting there like a very uncomfortable third wheel while he and Amber joked and shared a few quick kisses before Amber excused them for a round on the dance floor.

Watching the two of them kicking up their heels in time to the music, Katy couldn't help but wonder what she was doing there. Everything felt so *different*—*she* felt so different—it was hard to sit there knowing if she didn't get out soon she was sure to bump into more of her "old friends."

But wasn't that exactly what she had come here for? To meet up with old friends? To reminisce about good times gone by and to share the news of her recent engagement?

Unexpectedly, her stomach did a little flip and a wave of nausea hit her broadside. In a flash, she was on her feet, her fingers digging frantically into her purse for money to cover her drink. It was time to go. She didn't think she could deal with how drastically everything seemed to have changed. Not now. Maybe not ever. Slipping a few bills onto the table to pay for her drink, she cursed herself every step for coming back here as she made her way quietly to the door and the rental car waiting outside.

"Why do I keep doing this?" she whispered quietly to herself while she unlocked the car and slid inside. "First with Matthew and now..."

Closing the door, she put both hands on the wheel, sucked in a deep breath and blew it out hard before taking a moment to look around. The big oak she'd parked in front of was bigger than it had been four years ago, but it, at least was mostly still the same. So were the wide rays of sunlight beaming down through its branches, heating up every surface they touched with a natural warmth her feet itched to embrace.

She chuckled at that thought. One thing four years away had not changed was her love of nature. Sunlight and shade. Tall grass and cool breezes. Hot sun-baked dirt banks and cool, rushing water gurgling as it bounced and swayed over her bare feet down at Rumor Creek. Wildflowers and blue skies and birds and trees and sunshine...

... and an antique table for two set up under the branches of a tall tree, draped in white, laid with fine china and crystal by a sensitive, thoughtful lover who would never take it for granted that she was there with him because there was nowhere else on earth she would rather be...

"You lost?"

Snapped out of her reverie, Katy stared through her open window at a guy with bright blond hair and an even brighter smile. "No. No, I was just about to leave."

"No problem." He nodded and smiled again. "I sure do hope you'll be coming back soon, though. I'm Wyatt. What's your name, beautiful?"

Katy's smirk should have warned him she wasn't the type to fall for smooth southern charm, even if it was coming from a cute guy whose whole attitude radiated fun. "That'll do, cowboy. See you around."

Katy fired up the engine and waited for him to move along before backing slowly out of the space beneath the oak. Glancing once more over her shoulder at what used to be a favorite stomping ground, she sighed, yearning wistfully for a time gone by. Unfortunately, without the people she used to know and the feelings she used to have and the ideals she used to believe in, the Horseshoe had become nothing more than just another small-town bar.

Why had she come back here, anyway?

Again, the thought rose up to haunt her, and she knew she wasn't just asking it about the Horseshoe. She needed to figure out the reason—the real reason—she had packed up as few of her things as possible two days ago and hopped a plane for a whirlwind trip into her past; a past she had thought never to visit again. But ever since Tipton had given her the ring, she'd thought of little else.

Was that it? Was it because Tipton had given her an engagement ring? Or was it the haunting vibration of a death knell ringing in the background of her life—the same chilling sort of tone she'd heard the last night she'd spent in Vine Falls—that had sent her running from the new life she had created, the kind of life she'd believed she'd wanted, straight into the arms of the unfinished one she had left behind without warning four years ago?

As she pulled up at the fork in the road, the left one leading back to her mother's place and the right to a lane that tapered off into a dirt path that ran alongside Rumor Creek all the way down to the campground where she and Matthew and a few of their good friends used to spend their Saturday nights around a bonfire, indecision tugged at her from yet another direction.

The urge to go right was almost irresistible. Something inside her whispered a promise that everything she was looking for, the whole reason she'd come home to Vine Falls in the first place, could be found down that old path. In the depths of her soul and without really knowing why, Katy knew it was true...but she forced herself to ignore its urging and put on her turn signal for the left one instead.

CHAPTER 3

Steaming water sluiced over Matthew's body as he stood beneath the shower's stream debating whether or not to skip out on the bonfire tonight at Rumor Creek. If he ducked out, it would be the first Saturday he'd missed in four years, but he had a very good reason for not wanting to show up: fear.

Seeing Katy at the Horseshoe yesterday had completely thrown him off track. If he had to see her again, even from afar just one more time, he was afraid he'd do something he would probably regret for the rest of his life—like skulk around and listen in on all her conversations just so he could hear the sound of her voice.

Or maybe he would keep to the edges of the bonfire and stare at her all night, mooning like a love-sick spaniel, because he knew he would never get enough of looking at her. Worse, though, he decided, would be if he actually came forward and tried to talk to her because he had no idea what he might say. If their conversation followed the same path his thoughts had since he'd walked out of the Horseshoe yesterday, he knew exactly which words would roll out of his mouth and the most likely order: "Why did you leave? Are you home to stay? Will you marry me?"

Scraping the streaming water off his face with both hands, Matthew tangled his fingers in his hair and attempted to scrub away his frustration.

He was insane.

Obsessed.

No, he was already *re*-obsessed and she'd only been back for a day!

Hell, he even still had the ring he'd bought her.

Right now, it was lying on the counter by the bathroom sink alongside his wallet and the seventy-eight cents in change he'd had in his pocket when he came in to shower. If he ignored all the warning signs firing in his brain and drove down to Rumor Creek tonight for some fun and a few beers, he might end up showing it to her.

Nope. No, that wouldn't do. That would not do at all said the warning bells that went off in his head, alerting him to the fact that he'd started thinking crazy. Shutting off the water, he stepped out of the shower, grabbed a towel and tossed it over his head.

On the other hand, if he let his fear of running into her again rule his decisions tonight, wouldn't he be setting an unrealistic "must avoid Katy" pattern for the rest of his miserable life? He groaned and snatched the towel away from his face to scowl into the steam-glazed mirror.

"Damn it, Katy! Why are you doing this to me again? Why did you have to come back now?"

He'd thought he'd finally gotten over her, finally had a grip on his heart, his life, and knew where he wanted to go in the future. But then yesterday she showed up and shot his plans all to hell and back again and somehow she'd done it without even saying so much as "Hi."

Not that he'd given her a chance.

Walking away from her yesterday had been a bit symbolic for him, now that he thought back on it. Like when she'd left him four years ago, he hadn't said a word —he'd just strolled on out the door as if he hadn't even realized she was there. He'd thought it would feel good at the time, but all ignoring her had done for him was to rip his old wounds wide open again, leaving him bleeding and far too broken to bother with trying to staunch the renewed flow of pain. A bottle of Jack hadn't helped, either, but he had sure given it a try.

He'd ended up staying awake all night, propped

against the headboard of his bed, staring into the darkness while he tried without success to reconnect the newly popped threads of his life—at least in his mind.

"You almost done in there, Matthew?" his little brother, Liam, called after a quick knock on the bathroom door. "Mama said you had a call on your cell. Why'd you leave it downstairs so she could sneak a peek at it, anyway? I know you hate it when she monitors your stuff like that."

The towel he'd been dragging across his chest stopped moving. "Who was it?"

If his mother had looked at the screen, she'd mentioned who was calling. If Katy had somehow gotten his number and called ...

"Just Ethan," Liam told him through the door. "Don't you see enough of him at the bar?"

Snorting now that he didn't have to worry about whether or not his mom would ask him about Katy, Matthew quickly ran the towel over his legs and back, then threw it at the bathroom door. "Shut up, punk, and go find something to do or I'll tell Mama you've got lots of time on your hands that you could be spending out back at the wood pile splitting wood."

Three minutes later, he walked out into the hallway in bare feet and half-zipped jeans, almost running into Liam who'd been waiting for him and was now blocking his exit with his hands propped on his hips while he glared at Matthew through narrowed eyes. "Nobody splits wood in the spring, gimp."

Matthew quickly twisted up his dirty t-shirt and smacked him playfully on the thigh. "They do if they don't wanna freeze come winter, now move or I'm calling Mom."

After making a face at him which involved screwed up eyes and some tongue, Liam reluctantly left him alone, disappearing into his room to do whatever fourteen year old boys did when they were trying to appear busy while not doing a bless-fired thing at all.

"Twerp," Matthew muttered as he strolled along the hallway past Liam's room to his own—a room he would not still be residing in if things had gone the way he'd thought they would with Katy four years ago. If only she had stuck around long enough for him to ask her to be his wife … .

Pulling a clean shirt from his closet, Matthew tugged it over his head and dropped down onto the edge of his bed, resting his forehead on his palms. "Stop *thinking* about it, idiot. You're going to drive yourself totally mad."

Maybe he was *already* mad.

He seemed to recall hearing somewhere that talking to oneself was the first sign of insanity, and if he was insane, Katy had to be the reason.

But she wasn't the only reason he was still in his old room in his parents house. He could have moved out at any time after Katy up and disappeared. He hadn't, though, because his father had passed away that same summer, right after she'd left. His mother and Liam needed him, so he had stayed.

Last year he'd decided they could survive just fine without him, though, and he'd started looking for a place of his own. He thought he'd found the perfect one, too, but now ... now Katy was back and suddenly he wasn't sure anymore.

Groping around in his top drawer for a pair of socks, he sat on the foot of his bed again to pull them on and reached for his boots. Maybe he would stay home tonight —spend some time with Liam at the basketball hoop he'd over the door of the garage last summer. "Hey, Liam, wanna shoot some baskets?"

"Nah, James and Jimmy and Seth are coming over later. We're going to hang out and play some video games," his brother shouted back. "Wait, isn't this Saturday? I figured you'd be going out to Rumor Creek."

Yeah, Matthew had, too, when it was Thursday and Katy wasn't back in Vine Falls, and everything else in his life was still half-way normal. "I was thinking about staying home tonight."

He heard Liam's scoff through the wall separating their rooms. "What sane, red-blooded American male would stay home on a Saturday night when he could spend it with half a busload of beautiful, beer-buzzed, country-music-and-down-home-men-lovin' women?"

Matthew walked down the hall and toed open his brother's door. "Me. You got something to say about that?"

"Yeah," Liam answered without looking up from his hand-held screen. "You're an idiot. Now get out of my room, Matthew. Can't you see I'm busy?"

"Busy. Right," Matthew answered, his tone loaded with sarcasm. Turning, he went back to his own room to get his favorite blue-on-blue buffalo-checked shirt, which he shrugged into but left unbuttoned. Obviously, Liam wasn't going to be any help, so after closing his bedroom door behind him, he headed downstairs to get his phone and return Ethan's call.

Maybe something had come up at the factory and Ethan needed his help? A quick conversation put that idea to rest.

"I was just calling to make sure you're gonna stop by the church to bring the chairs. I don't want to sit on the ground again like I did last Saturday," Ethan grouched. "Man, I've got ant bites all the way up my legs and a few more in places you don't even want to know about!"

And so, for the sake of Ethan's scrawny legs and the other places he really didn't want to know about, Matthew got in his truck and drove the half-mile to the church to load up the chairs from the church's reception hall. He would drop them off at the creek, then come back home. He could pick them up and bring them back again on Monday. There was absolutely no logical reason he had to stay at the creek once he got there, he decided. And yet, for reasons known only to his quietly suffering soul, stay was exactly what he did.

Mostly because Katy wasn't there, he told himself ten minutes after he arrived. But that didn't explain why he stuck around to help unload and set up the chairs, or why he then kept hanging around, chatting with Ethan and Jensen and BobbyJoe until long after the bonfire had been lit. Or why he hadn't walked back up the hill, jumped in his truck, and high-tailed it out of there the minute he'd felt that tingling pull of awareness. Glancing with anticipation and dread across the blazing fire, his eyes confirmed what his heart already knew: Katy had shown up after all.

Dammit.

Had he been waiting for her?

There was no sense denying he had.

As sure as his brother's name was Liam, Matthew knew he'd stalled on purpose tonight so he could see her again, only it had taken until just now for him to realize what a dumb idea that had been.

What if she saw him? What if she wanted to talk? Worse, what if she didn't?

He thought about walking over, bold as brass, and

saying hello. But just as quickly, he decided against it. Being near her right now might prove to be too much. If he couldn't even get his thoughts under control, how in the world would he keep a leash on his mouth?

Cursing himself for a fool, Matthew eased backward ten paces, quietly slipping into the shadows where the flickering light of the bonfire's flames didn't quite reach. With one shoulder propped against the rough trunk of an old oak tree, he stood there alone in the dark, watching as she interacted with their friends the same as she used to do and once again he found it hard to believe four years had passed and just as easily disappeared the second she'd walked back into his rose-colored line of sight.

If he closed his eyes and forced himself to forget the pain of the past four years, he could almost allow himself to pretend she'd never left. Even from a distance her voice affected him; her laughter pierced him. Each pause for breath was one more significant nuance that took him back in his thoughts to a time in his life he'd really thought he was starting to forget.

The soft crack of a twig brought his eyes open and he squinted into the darkness around him while he waited for his eyes to adjust, and when they did, his heart thudded in his chest, beating hard against his ribs.

Katy. She'd found him out and was making her way away from the bonfire toward him. In fact, she was already too close for him to bear—or to slink deeper into the shadows and find a better place to hide.

His heart picked up a beat and he straightened against the tree trunk, suddenly feeling like a teen about to be approached by his long-time crush, and he couldn't decide if he wanted to run away or play it cool by holding his ground and trying to pretend he wasn't at all affected by just the sight of her.

In the end he decided attempting to be an adult about it was probably his best bet. Crossing his arms over his chest, he waited for her to get closer, to see him lounging there in the darkness.

Would she call him out for ignoring her the other day at the Horseshoe? Or had she even noticed him walking past her that day? Whatever her reason for seeking him out tonight, she was getting close—too close for him to make a quick, quiet escape and his body acted accordingly, subtly steeling itself for whatever cruelty she might have come over to inflict.

Mentally ticking off every second it took for her to move close enough for him to touch—if she was still brave enough to come that far—it occurred to Matthew that he didn't actually know the reason *why* she'd come back to Vine Falls.

At least twenty reasons he thought he could live with immediately popped into his head. Most prominent was the one where she confessed she had finally realized she loved him more than anything she'd left him for and had come back to pick up where they'd left off.

The idea of it made him feel good but he had a sneaking suspicion *he* wasn't actually the reason Katy had come back here at all—and she was almost directly in front of him now though she was too distracted by something in their immediate surroundings to realize it.

Instinct said he should pull her against his already aching body before she had time to remind him why he shouldn't; it urged him to kiss her senseless—the way he used to do—before she opened her mouth and tried to make perfect sense of their unexpectedly belated reunion.

Instinct made him impatient and eager.

Common sense made him cautious.

Well, common sense and the fact that she was going to walk right into him if he didn't announce his presence soon.

He was going to have to talk to her.

CHAPTER 4

"I was sorry to hear about your mom and dad." Katy offered the belated condolence as she walked down to the bonfire with Sadie Powell and Jensen York. LoraLynn had told her how Sadie's parents had been in an accident and died because another driver had been texting while driving and hit her parents' car head on. She'd also let it slip how bad Sadie had taken their deaths and about how wrecked she'd been afterward.

"Thank you. Going on was rough for a while and some things will probably never feel normal again. I'm a lot better now—except when it comes to cars and driving." Her gaze flickered to the man at her side and she smiled, affectionately nudging him with her shoulder. "Jensen's been a real lifeline."

Jensen shrugged. "Hey, that's what friends do, right?"

"That and share their houses." Sadie grinned. "You heard about the York place? It burned a couple weeks ago. No one was hurt or anything. Jensen's rebuilding, of course, but he's bunking over at the house with me in the meantime."

"Wow. Sorry, Jen." Realizing her comment could be taken more than one way, Katy's eyes widened. "I meant about the house, not about your shacking up with Sadie here."

"Shacking up?" Jensen snorted at her teasing and hooked a thumb over his shoulder, motioning toward a pair of chairs where they'd been set up in groups around the bonfire. "Oh, no. Not I. That'd be Miss LoraLynn and our boy Prater over there."

Murmuring her agreement, Katy let her gaze wander, taking in the faces of those present, both old and new. She didn't dare acknowledge that she was looking for Matthew, but her stomach did a happy little flip when she spied him lurking on the other side of the bonfire just the same.

"Lot of stuff has changed since you left, Kate, but some things are always going to be the same. Down here, friends are still friends and Saturday night still means *party* at Rumor Creek!"

Katy blinked, hoping her reaction to his use of the more grown up sounding shortened version of her name didn't show in her expression. Tipton called her Kate, but he was the only one. None of her friends ever had, and hearing Jensen do so was—oddly uncomfortable. For some reason, being reminded of her fiancé while hanging out with her buddies at Rumor Creek was unsettling.

"Pah-tay? Did I just hear someone say pah-tay?" Ethan Jones sidled over to ask, his voice at least three decibels over loud, but Jensen didn't seem to mind. Grinning, he turned and slapped Ethan a "guy five," which was basically a high five with a little head motion and music-less dancing in place before pointing Katy toward a couple of barrel-shaped containers full of ice that someone had set up by a tree in a clearing away from the fire.

"Drinks are over there," he told Katy before back-walking a few steps on his way to join Ethan and the others at the bonfire. To Sadie, he said, "You two grab a bottle and bring Katy over to say hello?"

The next thing she knew, dusk melted into full-on dark and though she'd been enjoying herself with her old friends and mingling with the new people, Katy still hadn't found a moment to ask about or speak with Matthew. Mostly because he'd kept to the shadows and partly because everyone else seemed hesitant to mention him at all, but she knew he was there because she could still feel his presence, and once in a while, the lingering touch of his gaze.

She had kept her glances into the shadows

surrounding the fire mostly surreptitious—just because she couldn't keep her eyes from wandering off to find Matthew didn't mean all her friends had to know about it, right? Still, no matter how subtle she tried to be, she couldn't seem to make herself *not* let her eyes linger on his silhouette a moment before roaming all over him every time her eyes found him in the dark.

What in the world was wrong with her? She wasn't supposed to be lighting up like a Christmas tree from looking at Matthew Shaw. He was her past. Tipton was her future. But right now, as she cast another furtive glance in Matthew's direction, she got the message loud and clear that her present was about to be thoroughly unsettled.

Just knowing he was there, outside the light of the bonfire's leaping flames, hidden in shadows so dark she almost had to squint to see him even with her glasses on made her skin tingle with a warm awareness she knew she shouldn't allow herself to feel. Even after all this time, Matthew Shaw affected her in ways she was beginning to believe no other man on Earth ever would ... and that was why she knew better than to seek him out.

With her being this aware of his presence though they hadn't seen each other in at least four years, actually talking to him would be a disaster. What would she do when he opened that beautiful mouth of his and spoke to her again after all these years? The husky timber of his voice would spill out into the chilly night air and flutter over her like a swarm of molten butterflies, warming her to her soul. His touch would pour over her and she would quiver with joy, welcoming the bliss of being rinsed with fire.

There was no doubt about it: whether from across a semi-crowded bar or a raging bonfire, Matthew Shaw drew her like a moth to a flame and given her present circumstance, he was the one person she knew she should avoid like the devil. If she so much as got near him, her breath would tremble, her fingers would quake with the need to touch him, and her entire body would unfurl in answer to his beckoning heat. So she kept her distance and simply watched him moving around in the shadows instead.

She wouldn't seek him out or try to interact with him in any way. Not because she didn't want to, but because she knew doing so would be a mistake. She was engaged to be married, and that meant Matthew Shaw could be nothing more to her anymore than a long lost friend. What she didn't understand was why she felt torn and confused inside.

"Hello? Earth to Katy? Are you still with us or have you been caught up in an invisible beam from the Mother ship that's come to take you home?"

The laughter in Sadie's voice had an edge that let Katy know she'd been caught drooling over her ex-boyfriend. Sadie had found her out and she knew she could no longer avoid the elephant on the riverbank. Pointing into the shadows, she said, "Isn't that Matthew I see hanging out all alone back there?"

Sadie leaned around her and held up a hand to block the light so she could peer into the darkness on the other side of the fire. "Is it? I'm not sure. Can't make out his features with the firelight blinding me. It *is* Matthew. No, wait. Could be Brae. I don't know. Why don't you walk over there and see?"

Katy knew they were all waiting to see what would happen when she and Matthew came together again but she wasn't sure what any of them really expected. She wasn't sure what *she* expected. When she'd seen Matthew at the Horseshoe, he hadn't even acknowledged her presence. If he'd decided to ignore her *there*, nothing was stopping him from doing the same *here*. Her face burned at the thought of it. Still, she nodded at Sadie and started around the bonfire.

It was quieter on the other side, although the music—as always—was was still clear as a bell; just like it had been during those late Saturday evenings when it was just her and Matthew and a few close friends hanging out here during their last year in high school.

Walking along the banks was a lot easier now, though, she realized, and she wondered who had taken the time to make this area of Rumor Creek so hospitable to humans. Back when she and Matthew and their friends came here, everything had been wild and prickly and natural.

She'd loved it.

Not that she didn't like it now.

Whoever had cleaned things up had made sure to keep the grounds and surrounding flora and fauna mostly as they had been. The main differences were the large circle of dirt and stone where the bonfire was laid and the once tall grass had been pushed back and somewhat tamed. Even in the dark, she didn't have to worry about where her feet were going. No snake fit to wear its skin—or rattles, for that matter—would dare wander into such a neatly manicured area.

Thinking of snakes avoiding this new campground/picnic spot on the banks of Rumor Creek merely because somebody had cut the grass (who did she think she was kidding? She knew Matthew was responsible) made her lips curl into a smile. Having lived in Vine Falls most of her life, she'd walked up on more than a few of those slithering, cold-blooded reptiles. Many a time she had waited, one foot in the air while she held back, hardly daring to breathe much less put her foot down, while a chicken snake, cottonmouth, or even a rattler or two wiggled across her path.

Her friends in the city would probably faint on the spot to see the kind of snakes Katy had seen every summer here at home. The only time they saw reptiles like those of her youth, they were locked safely behind the protective glass of their cages—the snakes, not her friends, she corrected her own thoughts then laughed when she realized what she had done.

"Penny for them."

Matthew's voice reached her before Katy realized how close he was and that she'd practically walked into him, and a quick, involuntary gasp slid past her lips. She'd been so preoccupied, noticing the changes on the creek bank that she hadn't noticed him silently walking up to meet her. Equally reflexive, her hand came up. She rested it on his chest but couldn't decide if she had done so to hold him back or to keep herself from moving closer to him. Already, her body was reacting to him. Her fingertips itched to move upward, over his chest and into his hair. Her palm was waiting in greedy anticipation to cup itself around his jaw, and her arms ...

Katy blinked, sucked in a surprised breath at her body's instant reaction to touching him again, and almost stuttered over her long overdue greeting. "Hello Matthew."

Snatching her hand away from his chest, she skimmed her palm down the side of her denim skirt. Whether she was hoping to erase the sensation touching him caused or control her urge to touch him some more, she wasn't sure. What she did know was that she wasn't supposed to be having these kind of urges. Not with Matthew. Not anymore.

"Hello to you, too, Katy. It's been a while." His hands buried themselves in the pockets of his jeans but she could feel his eyes on her. "I wasn't sure you'd come out here tonight."

Forcing a laugh, she said, "Are you kidding? It's Saturday night. Where else would anyone be but sneaking down to knock back a few cold ones and roast hot dogs on a blazing bonfire down at Rumor Creek?"

The half-smile that turned one side of his lips upward was still adorable. "True."

Their gazes met and her mouth went dry. Searching for something to say—something other than the yearning pleas her body was begging her to utter, she said, "This looks nice. I love what you've done here, Matthew."

And just like that, his gaze shot off into the trees, avoiding hers. He shrugged. "Thanks, I guess. The area is kind of sentimental to me."

Ignoring the segue possibilities his comment offered up, Katy turned and took a few steps toward the water, talking to him over her shoulder as she went. "I can't believe you got old man Peterson to let you do it, though. Remember back when we tried to get him to let us clean the place up? He almost had a stroke before he could manage to get his shotgun untangled from his camo while warning us the whole time that we'd better stay out from back here."

"Yeah, well." Matthew reached around his shoulder to swat at something on his back. "Darn mosquitoes. Anyway, what was I saying? Oh, yeah. Peterson doesn't much care what I do back here anymore."

That was surprising. Half her teenage years were spent figuring out how to get around Fenton Peterson and it had never been easy. The man seemed to have a built-in radar when it came to knowing where she was on his property.

"That's hard to believe. You'd have thought the man was going to take the place with him to the Pearly Gates. Wait—" she spun around, one hand on her chest against her heart while it thumped in horrified reaction to possibilities. "Don't tell me he's dead, too?"

Matthew shook his head. "No, he isn't."

Relieved, she moved even closer to the stream of gurgling water. Ignoring the urge to slip off her sandals and trail her feet in it, she looked up to ask, "So, how'd you talk him into it?"

Katy saw something flicker in his gaze before he shrugged and looked away. "I bought it."

She felt her eyes flare wide in stunned surprise. It was the craziest thing ever, but she was suddenly as excited as a kid at Christmas facing an entire tree-full of presents, all with her name on them. "You *bought* it?"

He nodded but nothing in his expression gave away even an inkling of a clue as to why he'd done it. "The grouchy old bastard wouldn't divide the parcel up, either. Said if I wanted an inch of it, I'd have to take every mile."

"So that means..." Katy let her voice trail off as she spun in a slow circle, looking around the place that held so many memories, some she knew she would never forget and others she wished she could. Matthew *owned* it. Rumor Creek—or at least this section where they'd played as children and where together they had become adults—was *his*. Had it really been so long ago when they'd lain together on a blanket not too far from here and talked about how badly they wished they could own it together some day?

"Matthew ..." Her lips trembled around the whispered breath that was his name.

He turned, his lips tilted wryly. "Katy...?"

There were questions in his gaze, burning questions for which she suddenly had no answer. So many things from their past called out, begging for a closer look. But she could no longer allow herself even a tiny little peek at them because...

"Matthew, I'm engaged." Holding up her left hand so the diamond on her finger could catch the light of the bonfire behind them, she showed him her ring. "I'm getting married."

CHAPTER 5

Matthew's stomach lurched.

Pain lashed through him.

Regret seared his mind.

A feeling of sudden but utter desolation almost brought him to his knees.

In the face of this new battery of emotional upheaval, his previous worries vanished one by one as his conscious continued to bombard him with a stream of vicious emotional shards that tore through his conscious to vivid awareness, each one churning and wreaking utter devastation on his already bruised and battered heart.

In this new, uncharted territory against which he mentally raged in denial, Matthew was thrown completely off balance.

Katy was getting married.

He should have expected it. Four years of absence was plenty long enough for anyone to prepare. Still, her blurted announcement left him reeling.

Katy was *getting married—to another man*. A man who *was not him*.

For a full minute—or maybe it was more?—Matthew actually felt like he couldn't breathe. He couldn't think. Couldn't speak. Actually couldn't ... *anything*. He simply stood there in stunned silence, staring open-mouthed like an an idiot, while slowly drowning in the deep, dark waters of painful reaction.

Luckily, his ego finally kicked in, saving him in the one moment he knew he most needed salvation. Crossing his arms over his chest, Matthew forced his gaze away to stare instead across the bonfire, his eyes pausing briefly to focus on one familiar face and then another to keep himself from looking at her. "Married, huh?"

A montage of images flashed through his thoughts of Katy in another time and place, happily married and loving life while he looked on, an empty shell of a man.

Each picture was another stab from the knife of misery, each vision of Katy happy and smiling with another man, with children that were not his, drawing blood until he felt like he was once again fighting to breathe and he knew he had to find a way to stop them.

He couldn't let her see how much her news affected

him, couldn't let her know how much he'd cared—how much he *still* cared—about her. Stuffing his hands into his pockets again, mostly to keep from reaching out to her, he said, "I'm actually surprised you waited this long, to tell the truth."

Only it wasn't the truth—at least not all of it. Heck, it wasn't even half of it, really, but he couldn't let himself think about what was. Looking back on every time he'd lain awake shaking and in a cold sweat, terrified that this exact moment had already come had been debilitating to say the least. Dredging up all those memories right now would only do the opposite of help, so he forced himself to ignore the pain and think of something else.

Cocking her head to one side, Katy peered up at him, her gaze probing. Questioning. Seeking. Only he didn't know what for and was afraid to ask until she voiced the question herself. "You're happy for me?"

Happy she was marrying another man? *Hell* no.

Matthew was so *not* happy for her he wanted to punch a tree. But he said nothing. Instead, he reached out for her hands, letting their fingers slide and loop together the way she used to do. For a minute, he simply stared at her, searching her face in silence while his heart flipped in his chest, frantically searching in the darkest corners for all its broken pieces.

Her expression became an odd, confusing mixture of surprise and relief and disorder ... and Matthew thought he might have seen something else in her eyes, but refused to let himself pretend what he saw lurking in her gaze might have been crushed hope or regret, or that it held a smidgen of disappointment and pain as well.

How could there be either—at least for her? She'd fallen in love with someone else while *he*—he had wasted four long years of his life waiting, hoping someday she'd come home to him.

His throat worked against the tight fist of regret that was slowly closing off his air until finally, he sucked in a deep breath and cleared it.

"Congratulations, Katy," he said at last, finally managing the words he'd meant to say before she'd interrupted with her question. But his voice sounded all wrong. It was strangled. Choked, even—cut off like everything he'd hoped for, dreamed of once upon a time, for his future and hers. He sucked in another breath and forced a smile. "I hope he makes you happy."

"Matthew?" Crossing her arms over her chest, she rubbed at her shoulders with her hands as if she'd just caught a major chill. She took a step toward him. "Are you okay?"

There was concern in her voice and an edge of something else. Once Matthew might have called it uncertain hope, but not tonight. Tonight, he knew without a doubt there was not one thing left in his life to hope for. Everyone else—all their friends, at least—had known it for years. He himself was just a little bit late, coming into the realization four years too slow.

"Good as I'll ever be," he assured her, forcing a casualness into his tone he definitely did not feel. Their fingers still looped, he pulled her closer, his eyes locked on hers. "Now that I have officially congratulated you, Katy, I believe it's customary to kiss the bride?"

It was a mistake.

Kissing Katy again after all this time was a big fat *huge* colossal mistake and Matthew knew it as soon as his fingers threaded into the loose, thick hair at her nape just beneath her braid. He knew it long before his lips touched hers. Knew it without a doubt when her body leaned into his, fitting itself to him as if she belonged there—the other half of him—and her breath slipped out on a wistful, whispering sigh.

But he did it anyway.

True, he'd meant the kiss to be a quick, congratulatory peck. A swift, meaningless meeting of lips to stop her questions, to give him a moment to gather his shattered bits and put together at least a semi-normal version of himself before he told her goodbye. But the minute her arms curled upward around his neck and her fingers skimmed into his hair, Matthew lost himself—again—in everything that was Katy Wallace.

The past four years melted away as if they'd never happened.

She still tasted like honeysuckle sweetness; her lips were just as soft as they'd ever been, but time and—dare he say experience?—revealed her to be more practiced. Shutting off the door to jealousy that demanded to know where and with whom she'd gotten so good at kissing, Matthew allowed himself to enjoy the fact that she didn't wait for him to show her the way. Not now. No, this time she met him fully in the middle, totally confident that she wouldn't fumble, wouldn't lose her way as she gave as good as she got, and God did she give.

With a helpless groan he deepened the kiss, framing her face between his palms before letting them trail down her neck, across her shoulders and down to her waist where they settled above the swell of her hips. He pulled her closer, so close there wasn't an inch of space separating them, close enough their body heat mingled, sinking through cloth and denim to settle against skin and burn its way through to his very bones.

This was Katy. She was his. His solace, the very essence of his soul, and Matthew knew without a doubt time would never erase her. Not from his thoughts, from his memories, and certainly not from his heart. Nothing he did or could think to do would ever be able to change the fact that he had loved this woman once—that he loved her *still*, despite the aching, regretful pain of knowing she would never love him back.

Giving himself up to the kiss, Matthew let it take him

where it would. At that moment, he didn't care where they ended, either, so long as she was still in his arms.

※

Katy struggled to regain some semblance of balance, some degree of restraint over her own body and mind, while her pulse continued to race blindly ahead until it finally skittered completely out of control.

Dear God.

The fire of welcome she felt with each sweet caress of his lips against her own both seared her and left her yearning—it was as if the last four years never happened. They were at Rumor Creek, they were together, and they were in love. Nothing else had mattered then and nothing else mattered now, other than the tumult of reaction she was experiencing in response to Matthew's mouth on hers.

Kissing Matthew was like being reborn.

His touch was both soothing and electrifying.

The unintelligible words he mumbled as his mouth moved from her lips to the sensitive skin just below her ear before moving back to her lips again were a promise, a whispered prelude to hour upon hour of unending bliss to be had if only she would say the word, and *oh*, so much more.

Somewhere deep down in a part of her she didn't

dare expose to the light of day, Katy knew she would never experience *this* kind of bliss with any other man for as long as she lived. Kissing Matthew brought on an enchanted sort of bliss, one she had only ever felt while wrapped in Matthew's arms. He was the only one who had ever been able to awaken such a response in her.

And yet, her brain began to remind her, reinforcing the rejoinder with a zinging little chill it sent racing down her spine. *And yet you are planning to marry someone else—someone whose kisses are cold, and detached, and more than a little distant.*

Plus, reserved and fleeting most of the time, she added to the thought, and at others even dull.

Like ice water sluicing down her naked back in the middle of a snowstorm, the shocking realization of what she was doing and with whom right now when she absolutely *should not be* poured over her, freezing everything great and wonderful about the kiss she and Matthew had just shared.

Her chilling realization came a bare instant before Matthew, too, stiffened against her. Freezing in her embrace, he lifted his head and shoved back, pushing her quickly away until there was an arm's length and a bit more space between them. Through narrowed eyes, he glared at her while he visibly fought to get his breathing under control.

Eyes wide, her heartbeat still tripping out of control,

Katy looked up at him in uncomprehending surprise. "Matthew? What—"

The furious glare he gave her then was murder on her newly re-birthed emotions.

There was scornful accusation also burning in his gaze, she noticed; a contemptuous disdain for her uncontrollably abandoned response to his kiss and Katy knew she should feel ashamed before he opened his mouth so that his harsh, angry words could confirm it.

"No woman kisses a man like that when she's about to marry the one she loves, Katy Wallace, and I know you know that—I don't care how long you've been away."

He was clearly disgusted by her reaction to him, and yet at the same time, he obviously was not unaffected by their kiss though he clearly thought she should be. She had seen his undeniable response in the way his pupils dilated, heard it in the harshness of his breathing. Could feel it in the tension radiating from his body even now.

Still, he was right—he was *not* her fiancé and his words just hammered that fact all the way home. The depth of her humiliation and wretchedness over her actions replete, Katy ducked her head and groaned.

What in the world had come over her? Had she not just told him she was going to be married soon?

And then there she went, kissing him with wild, unfettered abandon as if her very life depended upon it.

The damning act of her returning the kiss itself called her honor into question, but what was she to say?

There were no words.

What she had done was inexcusable and Katy knew no attempt she might make at an explanation would erase the recriminations she still clearly saw in his gaze. Nothing she could say to him now would excuse her body's unexpected but altogether natural reaction to his kiss, so Katy bit down on her kiss-swollen bottom lip and held her silence.

But there was something about the moment—or maybe it was the crackling snap of electrical fire still arcing between the two of them?—that made her suddenly stubborn, too. Yes, she had reacted to his unexpected kiss with shameful abandon given that she was engaged to another man, but she would not apologize.

True, she *had* kissed him—but *he* had kissed *her*, too, and Katy absolutely refused to be the one to lower her head in shame. Her chin came up and she dared him with her eyes to demand she ask for his forgiveness, or to try and explain what had happened when she was still reeling from it as much as he although a bit clueless as to why.

When she continued to say nothing, Matthew scoffed and turned to walk away. But he hadn't taken more than two steps before he turned back to say, "I think you should go home now, Katy. Go back to your mother's and think about what just happened here. Think about that kiss—*our* kiss—and then if I were you? If I were you, I might take a day or so more to think long and hard about those vows you're about to make. Could be you're about to make a terrible mistake."

CHAPTER 6

Monday morning rolled around and Katy was no closer to figuring out her feelings than she had been on Friday at the Horseshoe. Or at Saturday's bonfire. Or despite the fact she'd been conflicted by them all day Sunday.

In fact, she'd spent all weekend trying to come to terms with what had happened with Matthew—what she'd *let* happen—only nothing she did seemed to work.

Again and again Matthew's words tripped through her mind like a bad song she couldn't shake. More than once she found herself staring off into space as his words repeated themselves in her thoughts until it felt like she was drowning in them. But that wasn't even the *bad* part.

No, the *bad* part was she couldn't seem to find it in her to feel ashamed for having returned his kiss although she was sure without a doubt she was supposed to. Like Matthew had said, it wasn't right for her to kiss him at all when she was engaged to be married to someone else, much less with as much fervor and abandon as she had.

How unfortunate for you then, the voice in her head snarked, *that your fiancé's kisses never make you lose yourself the way kissing Matthew always did.*

No one else's kisses affected her the way Matthew's did, and yes, she had kissed a few guys. Rolling onto her stomach, Katy pushed her hair back over her shoulder and stared out the window, pondering the reasons why that could be.

She'd felt alive when Matthew kissed her—she always had. At the time, the way his kisses made her feel was just ... the way it should be. She hadn't thought about it beyond that. Not until he'd pointed out things should be different when you were in love, and he was right.

She'd always known love made things special between a couple but she hadn't equated kisses with a signal that something might be wrong somewhere if you didn't actually ... um ... *feel* them. Again, probably because she always had felt them with Matthew. When *he* kissed her, both Heaven and the Earth moved, leaving only herself and Matthew in the moment. But things weren't like that with Tipton. No, with her fiancé, things weren't like that at all.

Frowning, she sat up and bounced off the bed.

"Oh stop it, Katy. The measure of a man isn't drawn by his kisses," she reassured herself, repeating the words she'd heard her mama say hundreds of times over the years. And yet, the beginnings of a horrible suspicion grew that maybe, just maybe, it was. A little bit, at least. Otherwise, why would her reaction to Matthew's kisses when she'd never had the same with Tipton be bothering her now?

Nothing with Tipton was the same as with Matthew. Never had been. But that was how it was supposed to be. Right? They weren't the same person. They didn't come from the same town, have the same values, or even the same goals in life.

Tipton had goals—big ones. But Matthew?

Glancing out the window in the direction of the outskirts of town where she knew the factory sat, she shook her head no. Matthew had simply done what everyone else in this piss ant town had—he'd taken a job at the local factory and stuck his head in the sand. At least, that was what she assumed. None of her friends had mentioned anything to the contrary so she had to believe her assumption was correct.

Tipton, on the other hand, was somebody—someone important. He was a respected broker, a junior councilman, and a very necessary part of the community. In the near future, she had no doubt, he was going to be mayor.

But he obviously still isn't important enough for his kisses to awaken a response in his soon-to-be wife, the snark-voice in her head pointed out, making Katy growl in frustration.

"Time to do something constructive," she muttered irritably while bending down to search beneath her bed for her suitcase and then the closet for a change of clothes.

She was going out.

Amber and LoraLynn and Sadie might be working right now but by the time she finished showering and got dressed, they'd be headed out for lunch and Katy meant to join them.

After that? After that, she just might dig around in the barn out back for her old pole and go fishing. Anything was better than sitting alone in her room, talking with herself about why she shouldn't like one man's kisses when she was about to marry another and why she should feel guilty over the fact that she did.

But Tuesday morning found her doing more of the same. And Wednesday morning, too. She did it all again on Thursday and by the time Friday finally came around, Katy was exhausted but still feeling like a total fraud—and a fickle one, to boot.

How could she still have the hots for a guy she hadn't seen in four years? It made no sense, and yet, the way she'd practically gone up in flames when Matthew kissed her kind of said she still did.

What would be crazier still was if Matthew still had a thing for her, too. Four years was too long for someone to hold onto a love that had flown away long ago. No one in their right mind would wait such a long time for the one who'd slighted them to return ... would they?

Staring up at the ceiling, she frowned, considering.

Maybe *that* was why she'd come back home—to reassure herself that Matthew had moved on, that he wasn't still pining for her after all these years, because she just couldn't bear it if he was. If nothing else, Matthew was still her friend and she did not want to see him hurting because of her.

"Oh good lord," she mumbled to herself as she rolled over, flopping irritably onto her stomach on her bed. "You're being ten kinds of ridiculous with this *Matthew-is-the-reason-you-came-home* nonsense, Katy, and you know it."

The only reason she had come back to Vine Falls was to tell her mother—in person—about her engagement to Tipton and the upcoming wedding. Not once had she thought about Matthew or their past. Had she?

Looking back, she wasn't sure.

Groaning in confused frustration, Katy kicked her feet against the mattress a few times and then rolled onto her back to pout while staring in annoyance at the ceiling.

Matthew Shaw did not still have *a thing* for her, blast it! He was a grown man with a life of his own—one she hadn't been a part of for four years now. No way he'd kept a torch burning for her all this time, nor had she secretly held on to all the things she'd once felt for him, even if his kisses did still set her on fire.

"So why am I doing this?" she asked out loud. "I'm a bride-to-be and I should be happy! *So why aren't I?*"

The question only made her feel more annoyed and Katy pushed it aside. When she'd first come home, she had been happy, hadn't she? Yes, and perfectly fine. But then she'd told Matthew about her engagement, and he'd kissed her, and now ... now she was so conflicted emotionally she didn't know what to feel.

It's not a mistake, she thought. Marrying Tipton was not a mistake despite what Matthew chose to think. It was the right thing to do and she was doing the right thing, blast him—no matter what he wanted to believe. Only she knew Matthew didn't make accusations lightly. Nor did he offer up accusations when there were no obvious grounds.

He was honest; something far too few people were these days, and she had always admired that about him. He'd also allowed her to be herself with absolutely no thought of trying to mold her into someone who would better fit his life, his lifestyle, or his expectations.

Tipton, on the other hand, had taken her straight to his assistant the minute she'd said yes to his proposal and ordered a complete and total make-over. She remembered thinking at the time that he must intend to have the bevy of people waiting to do his bidding at the snap of a finger completely re-write the code of her soul.

Probing, prodding, re-engineering ... they'd even instructed her on the proper words to use when she told the story of Tipton's proposal. Not one iota of it resembled the truth, but as a man in the public eye, he could not afford to appear less than genial.

"What about less than human?" the snarkish voice in her head put in, and again Katy chose to ignore it. She understood public protocol was necessary, which was why she hadn't balked when Tipton told her he'd set up appointments for her media training.

He'd set up other things, too—things she hadn't really considered an invasion of her space and privacy at the time, but now ... now thanks to the delicious but forbidden kisses of one seriously sexy Matthew Shaw, she found herself questioning everything.

"Katy? Katy, sweetheart, are you awake? Breakfast is almost ready," her mother called up the stairwell.

"I'll be down in a minute, Mama," she called back and then pulled the covers up over her head, hiding beneath them with her temper still all in a huff. *Did* she love Tipton? Or did she still have feelings for Matthew? Did Tipton even really love *her*? Why *had* he asked her to marry him, and why, if she didn't love him as she had thought, had she gone ahead and accepted?

The questions spun 'round in her head until she felt completely disoriented and still they would not stop. Was it really her desire to tell her mother about her wedding—a wedding she had barely given a thought since she'd agreed to it—that had put her on that plane to come back home? Or, like the morning after the night she had spent with Matthew years ago, had the urge to come back here been just another Katy Wallace moment of cold feet and uncertainty?

Reaching blindly for a pillow with one hand as she held onto the covers with the other, Katy plopped it over her head and screamed out her frustration, something she hadn't done in years because it felt childish and immature. And yet, here she was, doing it again, and it was all the fault of Matthew Shaw.

Darn him and his ridiculous *what-if's*. *Ooooh!* The next time she saw him, she was going to give him a what-for he would not soon forget. Until then, however, she had to calm down and take a serious look at her life. *Was* she making a mistake by marrying Tipton? Could it truly be possible Matthew was right after all?

This whole thing with Matthew and her reaction to

his kiss was seriously bugging her, but unless she could find a way to sit down with him and talk, Katy knew she wouldn't find any of the answers she sought.

They had a past, only it wasn't *staying* in the past—it was popping up right here, right now in front of them and was clearly something they'd have to deal with before she could move on. But that meant she would have to see him again, and she wasn't at all sure seeing him again was a good idea. Just being in his general vicinity made her skin tingle with awareness, an excitement-laced, buzzing sense of anticipation she never had been able to ignore.

The vibrating buzz of the cell phone on her nightstand forced Katy out of her thoughts and back out of the covers. Reaching for it, she sat up and thumbed the screen to accept a call from LoraLynn.

"I'm about to head out the door for work but I wanted to call and make sure you'll be joining us down at the Horseshoe tonight. There's talk of bringing in a live band. I know it's not the art museum or one of those galas you're used to, but—"

Katy was practically humming with relief for the distraction. If she went with her friends to the Horseshoe tonight, she'd have something to do with her time other sit and think. "Yes! Yes, I am definitely joining you."

Sitting up, she curled her legs to one side and ran her

fingers through her sleep-mussed hair. "If I can find something fit to wear."

LoraLynn laughed. "Don't you go putting on no city airs with us, you hear? We are all the same old friends we used to be. You can throw on any old thing—if you still have old things to throw on. You do, don't you? One outfit, at least? How about that white cotton jumper you used to wear?"

She did. She'd seen it, still hanging in her closet beside the white silk dress Matthew had given her as a present before ...

The rattle of silverware on plates caught her attention, as did the smell of bacon, and something else. Something sweet. Her stomach rumbled and she tossed back the covers.

"I'll find something, I promise," she said to LoraLynn, "but it'll have to wait. I hear Mama dishing up breakfast downstairs."

Ending the call, Katy slid off the bed and walked barefoot over to the closet, letting the memories slide in as she went. The white dress. It had seemed so significant. In it, she had felt like a woodland queen—or a fairy sprite at the very least—a very beautiful and utterly feminine virgin fairy princess. She had worn it only once, on the last day she'd spent in Vine Falls—the last day of her life she could still see life as an innocent.

That was the day she'd given Matthew Shaw the gift of her virginity.

Everything had seemed so perfect then.

It wasn't until much later in that magical evening she'd realized exactly what she had done. Oh, not the sex. She'd known what making love was all about and she had always planned for her first time to be with Matthew. The sex hadn't sent her running for home, either, and then later all the way to the bus station.

No, it was the *expectations* she knew would come after that had truly terrified her.

"You coming down, Katy? The pancakes are getting cold and you know the butter won't melt if they do," her mother warned, prompting Katy to quickly close the door on both the closet and her memories as she spun around to find her robe and hurriedly belt it on.

Pancakes. The word alone made her mouth water and her stomach grumble. She could only imagine how they'd taste—it *had* been four years, after all, since she'd last eaten them and in all those years she'd found no one who could make anything that tasted as good as her mother's homemade pancakes.

CHAPTER 7

The past week had been a tough one for Matthew. Not that he would have admitted it if anyone had bothered to ask why he was suddenly so touchy. Luckily for him, no one had—not even the handful of workers he'd barked at or raked over the coals for the least little offense.

He'd thought going back down to the factory would help. Not that he'd needed to go. But when Katy had left before, work had quickly become his escape and this week Matthew had really counted on the day-to-day grind to chill him out, to put things into a clearer perspective. But not one chore or trial had come up during the week that was engaging or serious enough to keep his mind off her and the life-altering kiss they had shared over the weekend.

All week he had thought of it—relived it—and it was driving him crazy. Desires he thought were long since forgotten suddenly resurfaced, making him yearn for more even though he knew those desires would go unanswered because no matter how genuine or thrilling her response to him had been, Katy Wallace was now completely off limits.

Around here, single men knew better than to go around kissing women wearing another man's ring. An engaged woman was practically synonymous with a married woman and that was how he knew he should see Katy. His mind, however, refused to agree. In denial and determined to do as they pleased, his thoughts were suddenly operating under another set of rules.

A rogue set.

His thoughts were dead set on working out this thing with Katy and they refused to give up, even if where they took him made him look bad and they kept taking him back to Katy.

One kiss, and his was a mind gone wild.

But oh, what a kiss it had been. Hot enough to make him break out in a sweat and then do it all again in his dreams every night, that kiss had haunted him all week. But there was more to his surly mood than his reaction to a kiss. It had happened, true. And any man in his situation would have wanted to do it again—engagement ring or no. But what bothered Matthew had more to do with the woman behind the kiss than the kiss itself.

He was worried about Katy and how serious she was about marrying this other guy. Was she really sure marrying him was what she wanted to do? Did she even love the guy? He didn't think she did because—how could she respond so thoroughly, so passionately to him if she really was in love with her *fiancé*? None of it made sense and if it was off to him, he knew her response to him after all this time apart and while she was promised to another man must be mixing things up for Katy, as well.

Believing she still had feelings for *him* would make her unexpected reaction easy to get. *That* he could have understood. But if buried feelings were actually the case, the minute she'd responded to his kiss the Katy he knew four years ago would have backed out of it, admitted she'd picked the wrong man and whipped out her cell phone to call off the pending marriage right then and there.

This new quieter, more sophisticated and polished Katy?

Matthew wasn't sure, and the confusion it caused ate at him, making him surly and on edge, so much he'd been unusually bad-tempered all week. By the time he pulled up at the Horseshoe Friday evening, he was a full-on snapping, snarling bag of growl he knew nobody in their right mind would want to be around. *He* didn't want to deal with his temper himself. But neither was he going to let Katy's homecoming keep him from doing things the way he usually did.

Friday evenings were spent brooding in the shadows from the back table that had practically become his while everyone else he knew danced and had a good time—which was exactly what he was settling in to do when the male half of their normal crowd showed up and Jensen slid into a chair at his table about two seconds before Ethan and BobbyJoe joined him.

"Hey, man, guess who's back in town? You'll never guess," Jensen said and proceeded to answer his own question before Matthew could get a word in edgewise. "Katy Wallace. Remember her? You remember her. Well, she's back. I heard from LoraLynn. Well, actually LoraLynn told Sadie, and Sadie told me, and I ..."

"...told a few hundred other people, no doubt," Matthew grumbled. Jensen knew good and well he remembered Katy. As if he could forget her. But now his friends would all know he knew she was back and everyone would be watching, waiting to see what happened when the two of them came together.

Only they already had and his friends had missed it. But he wasn't about to tell them that.

"What I'm wondering is if you'll finally give up your permanent residence at the boob table and un-don the requisite ogre scowl you've worn for the past few years?" Jensen teased but Matthew didn't find the least bit of humor in his words.

Ethan did. He laughed.

"A girl as hot as Katy Wallace comes rolling back onto the grounds, won't take long for the whole town to know." His fingers thrummed on the table for a second before he pinned Matthew with a questioning stare. "But the question if I correctly recall, Monkus Matthew, was whether or not *you* knew she'd come home. Did you?"

In the minute of hushed silence that ensued, Matthew tried to figure out a way to evade the question. If he said yes, there would be expectations of an explanation. Something he definitely wasn't about to give. If he lied and said no, well, nothing good ever came from lying, as far as he could tell. On the other hand, it would get their eyes off him and the conversation moving along so he could go back to sitting in brooding silence as his friends had come to expect from him over the past few years.

Or, he could simply ignore their questions and ...

A desperate glance toward the door spoiled that possibility entirely. Jolted into hyper-awareness, he felt her presence all the way across the room. Katy walked in with LoraLynn and Amber, followed by Erin and Sadie and a few of the other girls he remembered from school—

her old classmates. *Their* old classmates. His mouth hardened into a grim line.

Tilting his head in the group's general direction, he said, "If I didn't before, I sure do now. It'd be kind of a hard fact to miss, given she's just walked in the door."

An area, he decided, which was no longer a safe haven for his gaze. Just before he opted to glare at the tabletop, he saw Sadie smile and wave before she looked pointedly at Jensen and motioned with a quick tilt of her head toward the dance floor.

"That's my cue," Jensen said, sliding out of the chair he'd just plopped into so he could join her for a dance before the games started in the pool room.

Matthew snorted. "You'd think there was something going on between those two the way they are always at each others beck and call."

BobbyJoe also excused himself and followed, holding out his hand in request for a dance with LoraLynn and Ethan quietly studied the pair before turning back to Matthew, an indiscernible glint in his eye that had Matthew bristling and instantly on guard.

Not that it would do him any good.

"You knew she was back, didn't you?"

Matthew nodded and rather than fish blindly around for an explanation, decided to go with the truth. "Saw her last weekend at the bonfire."

"I thought you dropped off the chairs and left?"

Ethan asked, but his speculative look became penetrating.

Matthew fought the childish urge to squirm in his chair. "Nah, I hung around for a bit. Did you know she's engaged?"

The words were bitter in his mouth but he forced himself to say them anyway. Might as well. Katy was wearing a ring now, one that was kind of impossible not to see. With his friends and their prodding questions, he figured it was probably best to go ahead and get everything out in the open.

"Yep. Heard that from LoraLynn." Ethan's brows rose as he leaned back in his chair and a wicked glint lit up in his eyes. "Does it bother you much?"

Matthew pinned him hard with a cold, narrow-eyed stare. "Not at all. Should it?"

Ethan couldn't hold back his laughter. Shaking his head in disbelief at how badly his friend had failed in his pretense, he said, "You're a bad liar, Shaw. A really, really bad one. Why don't you go ask her to dance? It's not like she's married yet. Right?"

Pushing his chair back until it was balanced on just two legs, Matthew reclined into the shadows but now, after Ethan's surprising quip, his eyes were doing a little scrutinizing of their own. Had the entire world flipped off its rocker when Katy came back to town?

"That ain't how it's done around here, Ethan, and I

know you know it, too. She's not married. I get that. But as far as guys like us are concerned, engaged means she might as well be." He tried to keep his voice neutral but the regret he'd desperately tried to hide came through just the same.

Ethan's shrug was casual. "Minds can change. Especially with a little help, and I'm game if you want me to give it. You were her first love, Matthew, which means this guy's second best from the get go and we all know it. Besides, who's to say it's wrong if somebody were to sneak in with a few fond memories and invite someone else—an old friend, say—to go on a merry stroll down memory lane that just so happens to give them a little nudge in the right direction?"

Matthew held his tongue, preferring to brood in silence over his own thoughts about Katy's engagement. What was it with his friends tonight, anyway? Had they always been like this? Thinking it was just perfectly okay to hash out the ugly details of people's past in public?

"Suit yourself, man," Ethan finally said. He didn't leave, though. Instead, he drummed his fingers on the table for a second time this evening, probably debating whether or not to shut his mouth and let things ride or keep rattling his trap until Matthew came over it and made a dive for him. In the end, he had more to say. "I think you're crazy if you don't at least go over talk to her."

He pointed in Katy's direction but he was looking at

Matthew when he said, "See that cautious, speculative look in her eyes every time she glances over here at you? Tells me she thinks the two of you have some unfinished business between you."

"And if we do?" Matthew's glare would have shook a lesser man. Ethan just chuckled.

"If you do, you'd best get to settling it, man." Straightening, he thrummed his knuckles against the table for emphasis, shrugged, and arched his brows high, which all served to make his parting shot more memorable. "Don't know if you remember or not, Matthew the Moody, but there are some things that can't wait until morning."

Matthew wanted to call foul on that one.

Reminding a friend they lost the love of their lives because they were so far deluded by bliss they'd decided it would be fine to leave their proposal till morning was a cheap shot.

A very cheap shot.

It hurt.

Not that Ethan hadn't known it would.

He'd probably planned out his exact words before he ever opened his mouth, and known just how deeply they would cut, to boot.

He was good like that—knowing just what to say to stir a hornet's nest or soothe a she-bear seemed to come naturally to Ethan Jones.

But Matthew wasn't Ethan, and more times than not,

everything came out wrong the minute he opened his mouth and tried to convey his thoughts with words.

Ethan headed onto the dance floor, leaving Matthew to ponder his words while, from his ogre's corner, he peered moodily out from the shadows, feeling a bit surly that his friends all seemed to be having a great time while he sat sulking over his own bad luck. Again.

Another Friday, another party seemed to be the motto for his friends. Used to be for him, too, but from the moment he'd awakened and found an empty space beside him on the blanket where Katy had been four years ago, all his parties since had been of the pity variety.

Maybe he should join them? Show Katy and everyone else he wasn't the surly ogre they all seemed to think he'd become after all? Maybe he should dance, too. Enjoy himself. Have fun, like he used to do.

Even as the thoughts chased around in his head, Matthew knew he would not be able to enjoy himself for real—not while Katy was here but engaged to another man. But he could probably get up and pretend to have a good time. Heaven knew he'd done plenty of that during the past four years. What was one more night?

Decision made, he grabbed his bottle and tilted it against his lips until it turned completely bottoms up, draining the contents in one long swallow before putting it back on the table with a loud thump. Resettling his chair on all four legs, he got up and did a little Swayze-style step-hip-sway jig before heading into the fray—one LoraLynn had somehow caught from the corner of her eye if the wicked grin spreading over her face was any indication.

"Woohoo! Over here, girls! Looks like the ogre hasn't lost his rhythm after all!" she called out over the music, one arm out-flung, a finger pointing in his direction.

"Those are tall accusations, LoraLynn," Ethan bellowed back. "Step on out there and let's see if he can prove it!"

Matthew knew he'd given her one of those secret, hidden cues of his because she did exactly as he'd suggested without question or complaint, making herself the very first in a string of Matthew Shaw dance partners for the evening, but not once did he ask to dance with Katy.

Whether he was with her or Amber, Erin, Sadie or LoraLynn, Matthew was aware of her presence in the room. He knew she was watching him, knew she fully expected him to ask *her* to dance, too, but getting close enough to Katy to dance tonight was the last thing he planned to do.

Dancing with her would be another big mistake, just like the kiss at Rumor Creek last Saturday—a grandly idiotic one he did not intend to make, no matter how much Ethan tried to goad him into it from the sidelines.

CHAPTER 8

"Hey, girl. Can I buy you a drink?"

Katy looked up from watching her friends on the dance floor to find the guy who'd spoken to her her first day back by her car hovering with a wide, friendly smile on his face while he waited for her answer.

He was a little on the young side, probably not much over twenty-one but something in his always smiling attitude made her think he might be fun if she took the time to get to know him a little.

"You're Wyatt, right? Suit yourself if you want to have a seat but I have a drink already." She lifted her glass from the table as a show of proof and then took a quick swallow before setting it back down.

A devilish grin curled his lips as he straddled the chair across from her, accepting her invitation to join her by way of doing just that, and sat his own drink on the table. "Well, now I'm right flattered. You remembered my name. But you never told me yours, as I recall. Care to rectify that?"

Glancing over at Matthew who was glaring her way, she noticed he'd switched dance partners again before she turned back to Wyatt with a smile. "I'm Katy. I'm not new here, but it's been a while, which would explain why you don't know me."

Wyatt turned slightly in his seat to follow her gaze and she saw his smile falter when his curious search for whomever she was staring at ran smack into Matthew. When he turned back to Katy he was almost frowning. "Uh-oh. So you're *that* Katy, huh? The one who broke his heart?"

Oh, that smarted, she thought, barely able to contain the wince his words caused. But she refused to be the bad guy tonight—or girl as the case would be—and declined to give an answer. Pursing her lips, she cocked her head to the side and looked Wyatt directly in the eye. "If you're looking for an all-nighter, you might as well know I'm engaged, and no, I am not engaged to Matthew."

Rather than putting a damper on Wyatt's spirits as she'd thought it might, her admission only made his smile come back. He even winked at her. "In that case, barring the arrival of your man, I might as well sit and talk for a while. Do you mind? Or would you rather be dancing?" he asked, giving a quick jerk of his head toward the dance floor. "I can handle my own on a dance floor and I'd be honored if you were by my side."

Despite herself, Katy felt her lips turn upward and a chuckle bubbled up from her chest. "My my, what a sweet little charmer you are!"

He grinned, showing off a set of dimples that would have any woman swooning and thinking up things to get him to show them off again and again.

"Yep! That's my middle name. Wyatt *Charmer* Harper." He leaned close then, eyes sparkling with mischief and mirth, and whispered, "Not really. It's Clinton. But I'll have to kill you if you tell anyone that."

Katy laughed and straightened in her chair, noting from the edge of her peripheral vision that Matthew was dancing again, only this time his partner was Gin from behind the bar. An idea struck her and she decided to test it out. "Well, Wyatt *Charmer-but-not-Clinton* Harper, I think your secret just won me over."

"It's always the secrets that the ladies fall for," he said, winking at her again.

"Lucky for me, I have a whole bag of 'em," he added in a stage whisper.

Katy laughed at that, feeling a little surprised she was actually enjoying the silly repartee they had going on. Without giving her a chance to change her mind in case that was what he thought she might do, Wyatt got to his feet and reached right over the table for her hand and said, "Let's go show 'em how it's done!"

By the time they finished their second dance and Katy went back to her table, this time alone, she had all the proof she needed; what she had suspected all along was clear.

Matthew was avoiding her.

Katy knew what he was doing as surely as she knew her last name was Wallace, and if what he was doing was so blatantly obvious to her, it was bound to be obvious to everyone else. What she didn't know was *why* he was avoiding her.

Last weekend, he'd congratulated her on her engagement as if he truly were happy for her. But now he was acting as if he were holding some sort of grudge for a past slight against him, only Katy didn't know which one. Was it that she'd kissed him back when he kissed her last week, or for leaving without an explanation four years ago? Whichever it was, his avoidance was beginning to stir up a lot of pointed curiosity and whispered gossip among their friends.

So he was angry with her. Fine. She got that. She understood it. Maybe even thought it was justified. But making their friends stare at them and wonder wasn't going to do either of them a bit of good—plus, it was only a dance, right?

One dance was all they needed to get through to put an end to the speculation and if he wasn't going to be a man about it, she, at least, was woman enough to do what she had to do. With one finger, she resettled the frame of her glasses on the bridge of her nose and got up out of her chair. If he wouldn't ask *her* to dance, she would darn well go ask *him*.

Matthew's table—*the boob table*, LoraLynn had called it, in deference to Matthew's attitude when he was moodily in residence—was tucked back in a somewhat private corner of the bar. It was darker there than in the rest of the place, which kept his expression cloaked in shadows so she wasn't really sure what he was thinking.

Katy felt more than a few pairs of eyes tracking her movements as she made her way over, though she did her best to ignore them, a feat she wasn't sure how she managed considering the fact that each stare felt like a heated probe boring into the back of her neck, making her skin burn and prickle.

With his features hidden in shadow as they were, Katy had no idea if Matthew had seen her coming—and she'd be darn surprised if he hadn't, considering everyone else's gaze seemed to be locked in place, riveted onto her—but she didn't bother to announce herself or to sit down once she'd arrived. Instead, she opted for what would have passed for normal—*past* normal—between the two of them if she hadn't gone away for a while.

For the sake of anyone who might have been listening, she purposely kept her voice light. The last thing she needed tonight was for him—or anyone else for that matter—to seriously create a scene. "Hey, you wanna dance with me? I know it's been a while, but I don't believe I've grown an extra foot or anything lately, so I should still be able to find my way around the dance floor, provided the music's good."

One look at the flinty steel of his eyes convinced Katy he was furious with her for daring to come on over after all he'd done to avoid her this evening. She could also tell by that same hard look that he was absolutely about to refuse. Then surprisingly, he shrugged and reached for her hand, and got up to lead her onto the dance floor.

Once there, he swung her around and into the fray of their friends, his body moving to the music alongside hers as naturally as if he were only breathing, the exact same way he used to do before she'd left.

For a fleeting moment it felt as if the past four years simply slipped away; it was like nothing had changed between them. Then, the song changed to a familiar, though much slower number and Katy felt Matthew go still. Her heart thudded against her ribs. Would he walk away and leave her there on the dance floor?

Fearing he would do exactly that, she quickly put her hands on his shoulders. Peering up at him, she leaned close and whispered, "Walk with me, Matthew. I think we need to talk."

Pulling away slightly, he nodded and asked, "You want to go now?"

She was tempted to say yes just to get it over with but something about the moment made her wait. She gave a slight shake of her head. "We'll go after the song ends."

Katy could feel the tension radiating from him, and not just beneath her palms where they rested on the suddenly stiff muscles of his shoulders. He'd gone rigid, and peeking up at him from beneath her lashes, she noticed his eyes were closed.

Rubbing her hands lightly over the corded muscles near his neck, Katy kneaded them with her fingers as she leaned in to whisper, "It's just a dance, Matthew. One dance to one song and then I promise I'll go. Relax."

When she leaned back against his arm to see his face again, his eyes had opened and were trained on hers, now penetrating and very, very dark.

"It's just a dance. Just one old song," he muttered but then his eyes changed and she felt the tension in him release. He smiled and her heart fluttered in her chest.

He grinned and she was lost.

"It might be just a song, but I remember more to this one, Katy. A helluva lot more," he said, his probing gaze searching hers in question even before he arched one eyebrow and asked, "Do you?"

"Flashlights," she murmured without hesitation, leaning against him now that he'd relaxed. Her tone went wry and her lips twisted in a slight grimace. "And a snake."

She felt his shoulders shake. "It wasn't a snake. It was a June bug, remember? But you didn't know that at the time."

Smiling at the memory, she let Matthew turn her around the floor, the two of them moving together almost without effort while she tried to recall all the details. "I can still remember the sound—and then the godawful racket of Ethan's big old truck barreling through the underbrush when he came crashing through to take me to the hospital. We all thought I was going to die."

Matthew's chuckle turned into a low laugh. "You'd already determined there was no way you were going to die by the time he got his truck through, though, and I'll bet it took a while before Ethan managed to wipe the image of you sitting there on my lap without your shirt on out of his eyes."

Leaning back again, Katy scowled and reminded him of her defense. "Hey, that thing was in my shirt, Matthew, and I thought I was in serious trouble. It was dark and anything could've crawled down from those trees with none the wiser!" She arched her brow at him. "If a snake crawled down around your boys down there, I'll bet you'd have been nude in a flash, too."

"Hmm," he murmured. "You have a point."

The memory brought a flush to Katie's cheeks which she cooled by resting it against his shoulder. That night was the first time Matthew had seen her breasts—and as it happened, Ethan, too. But sneaking down to Rumor Creek after curfew was always best done without wasting time and effort on a bra—unless it happened to be the one night a snake decided to take a dive into the loose neckline of one's blouse.

"That night was great, as I recall, but I wasn't thinking about snakes, Katy. Do you remember the first bonfire we lit on Rumor Creek? That was the night we first danced to this song."

She did. They'd spent the hour before dark stomping down the underbrush in a wide circle, one big enough to hold a fire in the middle and a few chairs around the outside. Ethan, Sadie, Jensen, LoraLynn, Amber and BobbyJoe was there, too, but she and Matthew were the ringleaders, as always. She snort-giggled against his chest. "Old man Peterson probably wanted to kill us for setting his pasture on fire."

Matthew nodded his agreement and when she looked up at his face she could see his smile had finally reached his eyes.

"We got into so much trouble back then. Remember when John Callahan locked us up for trespassing? And that time BobbyJoe let the cows out of LoraLynn's daddy's field?" He shook his head at the memory. "The entire herd, walking up the highway, blocking traffic for half a mile."

Like the herd of cattle he'd mentioned, a stampede of memories came rushing in, some of them making Katy laugh, while others dredging up a wistful sigh. There were a few poignant ones, though, that for some reason brought tears to her eyes—tears which she quickly blinked away. Luckily, they didn't talk about those. Those memories remained secreted away in her thoughts, far from the harshness of reality which, at the moment, she felt might tarnish them somehow.

Finally, the song ended and Matthew grew still again, his body once more tense and waiting though for what, she did not know. Stepping out of his embrace, she said, "We were so silly then, Matthew, but look at us how we've changed."

She attempted a smile. "We are both all grown up now, see?"

Katy let him catch her hands in his and swing them back and forth in a slight arc out to their sides while his eyes roamed over her from her face to her knees and back again.

"And at least one of us has matured very nicely, too." He'd tried to inject a teasing note into his tone but Katy couldn't help but notice his voice had dropped into a lower, more husky octave.

Her stomach dropped and her heart thudded hard against her ribs as she realized what that meant. He still wanted her. "Matthew ..."

Releasing her hands, he tilted his head toward the door. "We'd better take that walk now, Katy."

CHAPTER 9

The cool spring air outside was still a little chilly this early in the month but Katy didn't bother to stop by the car for her hoodie. Instead, she hugged her arms around herself and walked in silence at Matthew's side until they'd rounded the bar and started down the hill toward the lake.

The moon was already high and bright, lighting their direction. At the bottom of the hill, Matthew stopped and tugged her to a halt. "You wanted to talk. What are we doing out here, Katy? What is it you want me to know?"

So many things, Katy thought. There was so much she wanted him to know—too much. Far more than they would have time for tonight. She might never be able to say it all.

She wanted him to know she had cried every night for months after she'd left. That finding herself in a new place full of new people without his strength and ever-ready support behind her had been terrifying. She wanted to tell him the past four years hadn't been easy for her, either, and that he was the one friend she'd missed most of all.

But none of that seemed appropriate. Not after what had happened at the bonfire. Not when she considered the ring on her finger or the promise she had made to another man—one who was not even in the same state as her tonight.

"We didn't say much the other night. I feel like I owe you an explanation."

Matthew peered at her in a sideways look. "For kissing me when you're engaged to another man?"

"No." No, she couldn't even explain that one to herself, other than he was Matthew and she was Katy, and no matter what, when they'd touched nothing else seemed to signify.

"For getting engaged, then? Hey, you don't need to justify your decision to me," he said, but she could read it in his gaze how much he thought her having done so was a mistake.

"No, Matthew. Not that either." He might believe her engagement was a bad idea but she *was* engaged and he was right. She didn't have to justify her decision to anyone. *Not even yourself*, the voice in her head taunted, its tone intimating she couldn't do so if she tried, and she shook it back into silence. "I—I feel like I owe you an explanation for going away—for leaving you the way I did four years ago. And—and I need you to know I am really sorry. I left without saying goodbye—"

"You left without saying *anything*, Katy. Not one single damned word."

There was so much pain and bitterness in his tone, she winced. She would have had to have been deaf to miss it. "I hurt you pretty bad, didn't I?"

He crossed his arms over his chest and said nothing. The look in his eyes was damning and yet shuttered, keeping the rest of his feelings tucked safely away. There was pain in his gaze, too, and seeing it hurt her in ways she hadn't expected. But then, when she'd left Vine Falls she'd never expected to come back here, either. She most definitely had never meant to reopen old wounds.

Tears sprang to her eyes unexpectedly and she hurried to blink them away. Emotions were messy things and boy, was she feeling them right now.

"I loved you, Matthew. So much. Too much, maybe." Her voice was soft. Quiet. Regretful? "I think that is really why I left."

Matthew scoffed derisively but when he spoke, she could hear the anger and confusion mixed in his tone. "You left because you loved me? Come on. You don't expect me to believe you think that makes sense, do you, Katy?"

"You know what I mean, Matthew. Not *because* I loved you, Matthew, but because I loved you so much. What we had was great, but that was all there was for us—there was just nothing else. I felt trapped, I think. There was nothing to do, nowhere to go ... other than the bank, the library, the factory, or out."

The look in his eyes hardened and he clenched his jaw. Katy knew that if she were to glance at his hands they would be balled into fists at his sides. "I wasn't enough for you. Got it. Thank you for clearing that up for me. It's the kind of thing every man wants to know."

"Matthew, don't you see? If I had stayed ... I couldn't bear the thought of never knowing whether there was something else out there for me, so I left." He said nothing and she growled out her frustration. "Ooooh! Why are you making this difficult?"

"Just comes naturally, I suppose." He shrugged. "I did wonder why you went away. All of us did. Four years are gone and now look—here you are, showing up in our lives again. Back home, far more worldly, and engaged to a man whose kisses are clearly less than satisfying ... "

His tone mocked and Katy's eyes narrowed. "My relationship with Tipton is different."

Matthew's nod of agreement was not the least bit hesitant. "Yep. Clearly, unlike ours, your relationship with the new guy is not based on passion. So if it's not about the sex, it must be about the money."

Her eyes went wide. "How dare you say such a thing, Matthew Shaw? My relationship with Tipton isn't like that at all! He *needs* me."

Matthew nodded, but then he all but mumbled. "Can't tie his own shoes without you, no doubt."

With the derision in his tone urging her to lash out and hurt him the way he was trying to hurt her, Katy stiffened. "Tipton doesn't *have* to tie his shoes, Matthew. He has *staff* who tie them for him."

"*Paid* staff," she added before he could put words to the foul mischief she saw brewing in his gaze.

He didn't say a word, merely crossed his arms over his chest and rocked back on his heels while she went on a righteous rant extolling the virtues of her fiancé—never mind that they were all surface and superficial virtues. But then ...

"Why are you smirking, Matthew Shaw?"

"No reason." He pursed his lips and his gaze skittered away. "So ... you're basically his sleeve decoration, then?"

She was still so caught up in trying to find a way to explain all the reasons her relationship with Tipton was different than what she'd had with him, she almost missed his question. Almost. "Excuse me?"

"You know, a sleeve decoration. A fancy ornament he can dress up with and show off to his friends or use to impress his colleagues?" He continued to explain and then paused, one finger tapping his chin. "Wow. You're right, Katy. Love could never compete with something like that."

She glared at him. "You're just being mean now, Matthew, and I know you know it. I am not an ornament. Tipton loves me. Why else would I agree to marry him?"

Why else, indeed? The little voice niggled in the back of her mind, but she was quick to block it out and pretend she'd never heard it in the first place. Matthew, however, refused to let it go.

"Good question, Katy, but I confess I'm having a hard time figuring out the answer. I do know "the man loves you so you're marrying him" isn't it or you and I wouldn't be having this conversation right now," he said, reminding her yet again that he, too, had loved her—once.

"So, why don't you tell me, Katy? Go ahead and explain this one for me. Why *are* you marrying this guy? Oh, wait. I suppose sometime during the past four years you've discovered you like being the high-class equivalent of a hood ornament? Hell, if that's how you play, come on back up to the lot. I could pop you right up there on the front of my truck, and …"

His hands moved, mimicking the act of lifting her up

just like he'd said, and Katy couldn't hold back her fury. "Well at least I'd be moving up! And it sure beats the heck out of being the wife of a going nowhere factory drone who could never achieve a status higher than employee of the month!"

The minute her angry outburst left her lips, her fury and frustration disappeared, leaving her feeling suddenly drained and spiteful and childish. She hadn't intended to furiously spit out words so cruel and vindictively malicious but what she had said ...

Oh, for Heavens sake! Had she really spouted an excuse for leaving him that basically declared all she'd wanted out of life four years ago was a higher status than she believed he could give her? One glance at his expression, an expression that was at once both mocking and filled with thinly veiled disgust, said she absolutely had, only it really wasn't like that at all.

That she couldn't find the words she needed to explain and have him understand in the face of his determined scrutiny was frustrating. She needed space between them so she could think, could find the right words, but Matthew had gone silent again, waiting, and after a moment of not near enough time during which she gathered her composure, moved her bangs out of her face, and resettled her glasses, Katy opened her mouth to try and finish her explanation—to tell him why she had walked out of his life four years ago.

"That night on Rumor Creek—you knew it would be my first time and you made it beautiful, Matthew. Every second of our night together on that creek bank beneath the stars was perfect, but then you already know that, don't you?"

She struggled to find the words, to make him understand why one night of passion wasn't enough to base her future on, that—at the time—she had believed she needed more. "I knew you were going to propose. I even knew you were just waiting for the right time to ask me, and for a little while that night, Matthew, I fully believed I would be over-the-moon happy to accept. But then we both fell asleep, and when I woke up—"

His brow rose. "Did I snore? Is that what changed your mind?"

Katy shook her head and looked away, glancing off into the distance across the lake. "Freedom changed my mind, Matthew. I just wasn't ready for it to end."

Angling her head to peer questioningly up at him, she asked, "Do you know how cliché it is for people who grow up in small towns like us to marry right out of high school? To stay stuck in the same town and the same rut for the rest of their lives?"

He didn't answer, and she looked out over the lake again. "I didn't want to be that person. Not only that, I needed to find out if I could make it on my own. Graduation was barely over and for the first time in my life, I was free to make my own choices. To do what *I* wanted and I wanted to enjoy that feeling for as long as I could."

"I never held you back, Katy."

He hadn't. It was true. But if he had proposed and she had accepted, he *could* have and ... This was *so* not going the way she imagined, the way she had meant it to.

Every reason she offered for walking out of his life four years ago sounded shallow and immature, even to her, after her declaration of the truth that she had loved him. In fact, they sounded a whole lot more like excuses rather than solid, logical reasons because, well, she supposed they were. Excuses for the truth.

Why couldn't she just say it? Why was it so hard for her to simply tell him the truth and admit her only real reason for leaving him four years ago had been that she was afraid? Waking up in his arms, knowing the minute he opened his eyes he was going to ask her to marry him, she'd been so scared. Terrified, really, that if she had married Matthew four years ago she would never have had the chance to become anything more than she'd been at that moment.

She would have become a statistic. Just like her parents and so many of the people in this town, she would have been stuck in Vine Falls forever with no hope of moving forward or doing anything more than ... than anyone else still living here had done.

The very real possibility had been horrifying, so she'd eased out of his arms and ran like hell.

Leaving had changed something for her. She was different now. Maybe even better somehow. Wasn't she? Looking out over the lake, she realized that was just one more thing about which she was no longer sure.

"If you had woken up before me—" Her voice shook. Clearing her throat, she started again. "If you had woken up before me, Matthew, we both know you would have proposed and I would have said *yes*. I would have said yes and—and that would have been it for me. For *us*."

She was looking up at him, her eyes wet with suppressed tears and a real need for him to get what she was saying but Matthew was too furious with her to care. She had loved him but she'd left him anyway? Four years they could have been together, making a life for themselves, making children and beautiful memories, and she'd wasted it all on fear.

After a moment's hesitation, he reached into his pocket and pulled out the piece of jewelry he'd kept with him like a talisman against bad luck, probably the only thing that had kept him sane during the past four years. Reaching for Katy's hand, he pushed the warm metal into her palm.

"You know what? You're right, Katy. If you had stayed in Vine Falls until morning after our night together, I *would* have proposed to you. Hell, like you said, you might even have accepted, and then there you would have been? Stuck in the middle of Podunk, Nowhere without a lick of hope for any sort of high-class hood ornament status whatsoever, you'd have been exactly what you were afraid you'd become: another infinitesimal data point on some nameless, faceless stranger's chart of theoretical facts—just another jigger in a long, long line of *impersonal, irrelevant* statistics that had absolutely *nothing whatsoever* to do with me and you."

Biting off a curse, Matthew walked away, then turned back to add, "Since you obviously had no faith in me—in *us*—I guess it's a good thing you did high-tail it on out of town. If you'd stuck around till morning, Heaven only knows what other horrid sorts of statistical disasters might have been lurking in the shadows among the trees, just waiting for your "Yes" to happen!"

CHAPTER 10

He'd left her then, purposely ignoring her plea for him to wait when she finally did find her voice to call out. In the crisply cool semi-darkness, Katy stared at the sapphire and diamond ring in her palm while the tears she'd managed to hold back earlier trickled down her cheeks.

Matthew had bought her *an engagement ring*.

The significance of it was staggering.

A running joke in Vine Falls was that the engagement ring typically came long after a wedding—usually on an anniversary. For some couples, it came on the first one, but the norm around here was five. Mostly because the first four years were spent in financial struggle with both parts of the couple just trying to figure out how to survive. But not Matthew. No, he had gone out and bought her a ring before he'd even offered a proposal.

If she had stayed, if she had said yes, she and Matthew would have been the first ... the first to change things up, to have made a difference in the way things were done in this town, and God help her, he was right. She *hadn't* believed they could do it but he'd been working on it all along.

This was why he'd taken those after-school jobs but never seemed to have anything to show for his efforts. She wasn't sure how she knew but at that moment she somehow knew without a doubt he'd been saving his money for this ring.

For *her*.

How could she have been so wrong? About him? About them? About—everything?

The sound of an engine firing up in the distance drew her gaze back up the hill toward the Horseshoe. He was leaving now. She would be, too, but she'd left her purse inside with LoraLynn, which meant she would have to go back and bear the curious stares of their friends alone.

She wanted to be angry with Matthew for leaving her in this position but she knew it wouldn't be fair ... after all, hadn't she done worse to him when she'd walked out on him four years ago?

"Come on, you've got this one, Katy," she murmured

to herself, unconsciously repeating the phrase Matthew had often used to get her through the tough spots when they were younger. With the sides of her fingers, she carefully wiped the tears away from her eyes, absently hoping her eyeliner hadn't smeared. Red-rimmed eyes and ruddy cheeks were going to be bad enough without adding a raccoon smudge.

A deep breath helped to straighten a spine gone weak with remorse, and then she started the long walk back with nothing but her thoughts for company, weighted down by the beautiful sapphire and diamond ring she still held tight in her hand.

The sun had long since disappeared from the sky and now the night air was more cold than chilly. Spring might have sprung but here in Vine Falls, it did so in stages, with the heat only showing up every now and then. Shivering now, she hastened her steps toward the Horseshoe. When she finally stepped up onto the boards of the wooden front porch, she was surprised to find Ethan waiting for her in the shadows, her purse dangling loosely by the strap from the finger of his right hand.

"Saw Matthew pull out a few minutes ago and I thought you might be needing this," he said, holding the designer white fringed leather bag out to her like an unwanted souvenir.

"Yes, thanks. I'm such a mess now, I guess. I wasn't looking forward to going back in there like this." An awkward shrug was all she offered for explanation. "It's bad enough *you* had to see me."

Reaching out, she took the purse but didn't turn to leave. Instead, she hugged her arms around her middle, trying to warm herself while she worried over how to broach the subject to him of the ring and Matthew.

Finally, she just blurted it out. "Ethan, I've been wondering about something from way before. When we were still all in school, and—do you remember all those crazy after-school jobs Matthew had?"

"Yep!" Ethan grinned. "We used to give him heck for those. He always had to work when we could have been out having fun in the big trucks, slinging mud instead."

Her smile was shaky but she nodded, then cut him a glance. "I remember. Seems evil now, all the fuss y'all put up, but ... do you know *why* he needed the money?"

Peering up at him, she saw his gaze turn speculative while he considered her question in silence. After a moment during which he seemed to come to some unknown decision, he tilted his head to one side to watch her carefully, as if to better judge her reaction when he answered and said, "I do, Katy, and I'm betting now you do, too, or you would never have asked me that question."

What started as a sigh of reluctant admission ended on a tear-choked sob. She nodded and held out her hand, palm up, so he could see the ring. "I think so, but I need to be sure. Ethan, was Matthew working all that time just so he could buy this for me?"

After sparing barely a glance at the delicate piece of jewelry on her palm, Ethan tipped his chin upward to peer at her through narrowed lids. "Yep. An engagement ring. Oh, wait a minute, Katy. You mean to tell me all that stinking work he did—that was all for *you*?"

Crossing his arms over his chest, he leaned back against a post, a new, teasing glint sneaking into his eyes while he pretended for all the world to be belatedly offended. "Well now I think I'm mad about it and I have a bone to pick with you. No girl comes between a man and his dudes, Katy. Not in high-school. That's just wrong and you *know* you know it—don't bother trying to deny it. You *do*."

Even in the face of her misery, his pretense at being offended was funny. Her laugh was all warbled and still a little choked but she still managed a miserable little nod and a somewhat wrecked-up grin. "You can't hold it against me, though, Ethan. If you'll recall, I got out of your way real soon."

"Too soon, maybe?" he quietly asked, but he was giving her one of those curious, speculative looks of his again, and Katy had a feeling he already knew her answer.

"Four years is a long time, Ethan." Her gaze dropped to the ring in her hand, then she closed it and showed him the one on her finger. "A lot can change in four years."

Pushing off the post, he straightened and stretched before giving her a consoling pat on the shoulder. "Yeah, but lots of things stay the same, too, Katy. Heck, you might even find lots of people's feelings do, too. And a ring? Well, that's not really the same as an *I do*, is it?"

Without waiting for her to answer, he patted her arm again and stepped around her toward the door to the bar, his parting words floating back to her over his shoulder. "Nope, we both know a ring's not an *I do* a'tall, but maybe one of us should give it some more thought, huh?"

※

Conflicting emotions played tug of war with Katy's insides all the way home while Ethan's words pulled her thoughts back and forth in her head but neither side seemed to have an advantage.

Why did everything in her life suddenly feel so complicated?

When she'd decided to come back here for a visit before settling into the months of planning the huge wedding Tipton's mother had suggested, not once had she expected to doubt the soundness of her decision, and doing so was making her feel way too petulant and whiny.

By the time she pulled into the drive of her childhood home and made it up to the front door of the house she was furious about what Matthew had said to her about what she was to Tipton all over again.

Recalling his declaration that she was nothing more than a hood ornament on a car that was the arm of Tipton Van Warner the Third had set off showers of angry fireworks inside her so hot her eyes were probably throwing off sparks of total fury. Slamming the car door as hard as she could, she practically ran to the porch.

Barely pausing long enough to unlock the door, she set off at a furious pace again, stomping all the way up the stairs to her old room where she yelled into the empty space waiting for her there before flinging herself onto her stomach across the bed. "It's not true. Tipton loves me! I know he does!"

Only she had a feeling she'd yelled it into the room when no one else was around to listen because the only person she needed to convince she was telling the truth was no one other than herself. Lifting her left hand toward the light, she scowled at the sparkling diamond on her finger then reached into the back pocket of her jeans, digging around for the other.

"He loves me," she muttered crossly to herself. "He did ask me to marry him, after all."

Which was true but she knew whether or not she'd been asked wasn't the cause of her dilemma right now.

"He loves me, right?" she asked the ring, then reached for a pillow to wrap her arms around but the ring didn't answer, so she answered herself instead. "Of course. Of course. Of course he does!"

She stared at the ring, her brow pulled down in a taut little frown, and whispered into the room again. "But the question is do I really love him?"

From the moment she'd come home, not one thing had gone the way she'd thought it would. Right now she should have been ecstatic—no, blissfully happy! Ridiculously in love and all that jazz. But she didn't *feel* the least bit delighted. She was conflicted and confused, uncertain and ... and *moody*. Yeah, she was grumpy and moody instead.

For a woman who was supposedly about to be happily married, Katy felt curiously remarkably un-that ... and she knew exactly where to place the blame, blast Matthew Shaw's infuriating hide.

"You're being childish, Katy. Just go ahead and say it," she muttered aloud. But it wasn't her fault that every time she and Matthew came together, he made her question her decision to get married even more. Not that he should be able to. She shouldn't even care because—what did *he* know about a man he'd never met, anyway? What did he even really know about *her*?

"Nothing," she snapped sarcastically, rolling smartly onto her back. Only she knew *that* wasn't true, either, because he probably knew her better than anyone.

Matthew knew she liked it when he nuzzled her nape in just that spot while she was trying to read a book. He knew she was helpless to resist when he smiled that sexy, crazily crooked smile of his and gave her the patented Shaw pleading look.

But more than that, he knew *her*. The *real* her, not the one she had tried to pretend to be when she hopped a few states away and tried to create a new life—a fake one. At least it felt fake when she looked back on it now, and that shook her. When she left here again—and she would be leaving soon to go back to her *fiancé*—how would she know which was real?

A sigh slipped from her before she realized it because she knew Matthew Shaw knew her like no other person did. Tipton had secretaries and assistants to remind him of important days like birthdays and anniversaries and holidays and the like, but Matthew remembered on his own the anniversary of the death of her strange pet rock and so many other Very Important Dates in her life that mattered only to her.

Would it have been so terrible to have stayed in Vine Falls after all?

If she had, she would be Mrs. Matthew Shaw right now instead of the confused and inexplicably unhappy future bride of Tipton Van Warner the Third. Had she missed out on more by leaving Matthew under the stars that night than she could ever hope find with Tipton?

Still deep in thought, Katy twisted the heavy engagement ring weighting down her finger and it was only after she had done it that she realized she'd pulled Tipton's ring off, slipped it into her back pocket, and put Matthew's on in its place instead.

The simple diamond-studded sapphire heart should have paled in comparison to the gaudy display of glittering rock from her fiancé but strangely enough it did not. Matthew's ring seemed far more elegant seated on her slender finger and it felt perfectly right being there. But Katy knew she couldn't keep it—she was engaged to Tipton now, and this ring belonged to Matthew; the same, she was suddenly afraid, as did her yearning heart.

Scowling at the implications of *that*, she rolled off the bed and walked to the window overlooking her mother's back yard. Pushing back the curtain, she looked down over the lawn where she and Matthew and the rest of their gang used to play touch football in the afternoons after school when they were kids.

This time, without Matthew's urging, she wondered again if marrying Tipton would be a mistake, one worse than she once had thought staying in Vine Falls would have been—and it frightened her to think it really might, but ...

How did one even begin start over with their life —*again*?

With a sinking feeling that doing so would be much harder for her this time, she dropped the curtain and went back to lie on the bed.

For her and Matthew at least she was pretty sure four years was far too late to try and go back. Right now she knew the best she could hope for was that she and Matthew could still be friends.

CHAPTER 11

Rumor Creek on a Saturday night had a cadence all its own: friendly laughter, dancing, the low murmur of occasional conversation, and the ever-present thrum of music playing in the background made the creek side clearing come alive, but tonight Matthew only half-listened to the sounds making up a surprisingly fitting soundtrack for his thoughts.

With both hands tucked deep in his front pockets to ward of the cold, his legs were crossed at the ankles while he leaned his back against the bark of the biggest, burliest, gnarled oak still standing in the area. Far enough from the fire to be mostly hidden in the shadows, he spent his time scanning the small crowd either standing, sitting, or dancing by the bonfire hoping one of them would be Katy. But, the same as every other time tonight when he'd looked for her and had to accept that she wasn't there, the fingers of his right hand stretched and flexed in his pocket, unconsciously searching for calm in a riotous moment of dark disappointment for the ring that was no longer there.

Katy had the ring now. He had given it to her. It was the second dumbest move he'd ever made in his life—the first being to fall asleep with her resting sweetly in his arms before asking her to be his bride.

What had possessed him to give it to her, anyway? The woman was *engaged* already. The last thing she needed was another ring—especially *his* ring, and definitely not after all this time. Maybe subconsciously he'd just wanted her to have it? After all, it was always meant to be hers. But that was before, when he'd believed *she* would be his, and that they would be together for the rest of their lives.

In the background, the song changed to one about someone finally getting over getting over someone else and moving on with their lives and Matthew knew he should be doing the same. There was no reason for him to hope she'd come back to him anymore. Katy had come home but she was engaged. He had to let her go; he knew it was time to move on with his life.

The problem was he didn't know *how*.

The four years she'd been gone, he had clung to an unreasonable hope which the ring he'd bought for her and kept with him always had helped to keep alive. Now both Katy and the ring were gone; he'd never felt more alone in his life and he didn't know how he would survive.

He was so damned lost without her.

Swallowing hard against the knot of emotion tightening his throat, Matthew glanced back toward the bonfire. Watching his friends having fun as usual and enjoying the moment, each of them going on with their lives as though nothing were wrong while he stood alone and cold in the deepest of shadows was worse than sad—it was downright pitiful and he knew it was time to face the facts.

Pining for a lost love long after what they'd had was over was both ridiculous and more than a little juvenile. It didn't matter that he'd spent the past four years waiting for Katy's return—she was never going to be his again.

At that moment, he wished she had never come home. Wished he had never seen her again in his life. From the moment she'd shown back up in Vine Falls, all the progress he'd made toward learning to live without her had immediately gone up in smoke. Four years, up in flames. Incinerated—like his common sense had been the other night after they'd kissed.

Was that the reason she hadn't come down to the creek tonight? Was she afraid of what might happen if he tried to kiss her again? No, she wouldn't think that—not after he'd given her the ring, for sure. But what if it were true? Was it possible Katy was as unsure about her engagement now as she had been about him years ago? If so, maybe Ethan suggesting he remind her what being with him was like wasn't the wrong way to go after all.

The song changed again and Matthew shifted his position, trying to get a grip on his present but it was too tangled up in his past. Knowing Katy was in town, so close but so far out of his reach, was slowly killing him and filling him with frustration. His continued longing and undiminished desire for her served to prove he wasn't nearly as over her as he'd thought—and yes, somehow he'd really believed he had finally managed to start moving on with his life, to go forward without her.

Now? For the second time in his life, Katy Wallace was messing him up real bad. She was tearing him up inside. *Why* did he keep waiting for her? Not just in the past. He was waiting for her even now. Would he wait for her the rest of his life? Sadly, he was afraid he might.

Twice tonight he'd gone back to his truck, intending to leave both times. The first time he'd come back, he'd stopped by the fire to talk with LoraLynn and BobbyJoe, letting everyone assume he'd just answered a call of nature before he'd disappeared into the shadows again where he could keep an eye out for Katy's arrival or be alone with his thoughts if she did not.

The second time he'd turned around at his tailgate

and walked back down, he'd waited until he was far enough into the firelight for his friends to see him shrugging into his jacket—he had grabbed it out of the back of his truck at the last minute when he'd decided to go back to the bonfire just in case Katy decided to pop in late.

If anyone had asked where he'd been or why, he'd use the cold for an excuse—he'd gone back to the truck to get his jacket. But for all his unnecessary excuses it had been past late then, was even later now, and she still hadn't crossed his line of sight.

It was after ten when he finally decided Katy wasn't going to put in an appearance at all. He'd waited, staying a lot longer than he'd intended anyway, but she'd never showed up and now everyone else was starting to pack up, getting ready to leave, and when the music abruptly stopped Matthew knew it was time to give up and go home.

Pushing off the tree with one foot, he moved out of the shadows and into the dimly flickering light of what was left of the fire, thinking the moment felt strangely symbolic—not only as an end to the routine Saturday night but for all that had once been right in his life.

"Bum night?" Ethan asked as he walked out into the low light. Matthew's shrug was noncommittal. Reaching for a bucket as the rest of the group made their way toward the treeline and the empty field where they'd parked their cars, Matthew helped Ethan and the rest of the guys pour sand on the coals to finish extinguishing the fire. Cleanup never did take long and soon, even that part of the night was over.

After they'd gathered the bags from the trash cans sitting here and there, Ethan and BobbyJoe headed toward the treeline, too, leaving him alone with the night. He was in his truck with the engine started but in no hurry to actually leave when Ethan walked up and pecked on his window, motioning in the air with his cell phone, and Matthew pushed the button to let the window down to see what he wanted.

"Almost forgot I had something to show you."

He turned the phone toward Matthew, urging him to look at the screen and Matthew heard his low chuckle when, after only a slight hesitation, he reached across to the passenger seat. A few taps later and he'd added a contact, tossed his phone in the seat again, and turned back to Ethan to tip his head in a gesture of both acknowledgment and thanks. "Appreciate it, man. I owe you one."

"Yep. Later man," was all Ethan said before rapping his knuckles against the side of the truck in a kind of man-signal for "it's all good and you can go ahead and leave," then he turned on his heel and walked away. Through the rear view mirror, Matthew watched him go before sneaking a glance toward the back-lit screen beckoning from the seat beside him.

In a matter of seconds, he'd committed the number to memory, but still he didn't leave. For several minutes, he just sat there—engine running and his hands in his lap—wondering how long it would be before he broke and gave Katy yet another ring.

As it turned out, he was really proud of himself. He managed to wait three whole days. Work had cut off early and the sun was out in full force, making the early spring afternoon feel more like his favorite by-gone days of mid-summer, and as always, he thought of Katy.

During his drive home, he could think of little else but how today reminded him an awful lot of the last day he and Katy had spent together before she'd left and the picnic they had shared—and *that* got him thinking again about what Ethan had suggested—a purposeful trip down memory lane to remind Katy of how good things had been between them back in the good old days.

Sun, fun, love and laughter—just the two of them down on the creek bank with a basket full of food and a blanket where they could wile away an hour or two under the bright, baking rays of sunlight shining down ...

Inviting Katy for a picnic, he decided, was the best idea he'd had since she'd come back. Still, he knew he shouldn't do it. At home, he pulled up, got out of the truck, and walked around to the passenger's side. Before he even consciously registered what he was doing, he took out his phone, found the number he wanted, and quickly pressed the green call button before he could change his mind.

Katy answered on the fourth ring.

"How long has it been since you went on a picnic? Like way down in the woods, off the back side of a corn field?" Matthew blurted the instant she answered. Then he'd waited through countless seconds of silent agony in fear of what her response might be.

※

He sounded so much like the old Matthew when he called—the happy-go-lucky, fun-loving, easy-going man she used to know—Katy laughed in surprise and answered honestly before she had a chance to think about her reply, to possibly catch herself and what her glad tone might be revealing, and responded in the same friendly vein.

"I'd say about four years. Why? You have an empty blanket to fill?" In the heartbeat of silence while she waited for his yes, she realized he'd called her cell although she specifically had not given the number to him. She had only given it to LoraLynn. "And how did you get my number?"

"Ethan. He gave it to me, and yes, I do. Plus I've got a basket of food so full I know I'll never be able to eat it all by myself. Knocked off work a little early today, and it's nice out right now. I thought a couple hours of lazing around on the creek like we used to do would be great. What say you and I sneak off to that little place on Rumor Creek back where all the tall oaks grow? We can have lunch and dip our bare toes in the water while it's actually warm outside."

Though her whole body thrilled in eager anticipation, Katy knew she should refuse. Both times she'd been alone with Matthew since her return, everything had gone pretty much haywire. They had kissed. They had argued. He had even given her an engagement ring, but he was not the man she intended to marry.

At the same time, he was still her friend—always had been. She was torn by indecision. There were still too many unresolved issues—emotional ones—between them for a day out alone together to be anything even close to okay. Katy knew heeding her first instinct after her return would probably be her safest bet—she needed to avoid Matthew Shaw like the plague.

Opening her mouth to make an excuse, she was surprised to hear herself saying, "Will half an hour be okay?"

Having made the promise to join him, Katy's pride would not allow herself to renege although she debated the breadth of her sanity and her spur of the moment decision throughout the entire drive down.

He'd asked her to lunch, for crying out loud—a

couple hours of eating and talking. If she were honest, she would have to admit she would really like to catch up with him on what he'd been doing with his life. Besides, she was a big girl now. She could handle herself and Matthew, if needed, though she knew Matthew would never push her to do anything she didn't want—it was only herself she needed to worry about.

Pushing her fears away, she made the turn to Rumor Creek, chastising herself for acting so silly. Sure, she'd be with Matthew but they were only having lunch. There was no need to be so concerned over something that had both happened and been forgotten years ago by both of them. At least that was what she told herself, only the minute she set foot in the clearing where they'd spent their last night together before she'd left Vine Falls, Katy felt like she'd stepped back four years in time and their past had all happened yesterday.

When Matthew turned from laying out food on a checkered blanket to look up at her with a smile, she knew she was in trouble. Old memories rushed to the fore and no matter how diligently she tried to push them back, she couldn't seem to make them stop. The present all but disappeared, leaving the past in its place, and her eyelids drifted shut as she remembered every sweetly romantic, painfully poignant, and surprisingly vivid minute of it.

Food and sun, music and shade, the soothing trickle

of water in motion over the rocks below the creek bank—every wonderful moment had been punctuated by bliss, all in the company and arms of the man of her dreams. Life could not possibly have been more perfect.

Why couldn't Tipton be more like him?

Her traitorous thoughts shifted wistfully and she snapped open her eyes again, shoving the disloyal bits of wishful thinking away. Looking around while she frantically tried to find something safe and neutral to say, her eyes spied the old rope swing hanging from a thick branch in one of the tall oak trees. "Oh, you kept the swing!"

"That's a new one, actually. The old one broke." Matthew's shrug was apologetic. "Liam and his friends kind of overwhelmed the original one last summer. They get a kick out of coming down here to cool off and play."

"It's not hard to imagine why. I've really missed this place," she admitted, dropping down to sit beside him. "I can't remember a day in my childhood when I didn't spend at least a few minutes down here by the water somewhere."

CHAPTER 12

After lunch, Katy lay back beside Matthew on the quilt he'd spread on the ground earlier, making sure to keep a decent amount of space between them while they relaxed and let their food settle. For a long while both of them simply lay there staring silently into the sky, each thinking their own thoughts as the afternoon sun spilled down around them.

"You still love this place, don't you?" Matthew asked after a bit and Katy turned her head to find him propped up on one arm, staring down at her as he waited for her to answer the question.

"It's beautiful, but not as nice as I remember it being in summer. Remember when we used to come down here to work on clearing away all the underbrush but wound up spending most of the day splashing around and cooling off in the creek?"

"Yep," he said on a sigh as he lay back down, this time with his hands behind him so he could use them as a pillow for his head. "Then afterward, we would lay on the ground just like this and try to find things up in the clouds."

Soon they were doing just that—watching the clouds, picking out different pictures and silly little shapes and laughing over what they each thought they saw, just the way they used to.

"Look at that one over there," Matthew pointed at a particularly bulky and misshapen cloud. "I think it looks like a gorilla."

"No, it looks like a big old mountain to me. Oh, wait, I think I see a tail."

"Gorillas don't have tails. They have big red a—"

"That's *baboons*, Matthew!" Katy laughed and then nudged him with her shoulder. "And don't you dare even go there."

"Why not? Gorillas have a right to be in the clouds if they want to. Look, I think I see some more of them over there. A whole entire gorilla family, sitting and picking the fleas and ticks off each other—I hear it makes for a scrumptious gorilla family lunch. I wonder if they have picnics like we do?"

Turning her head slightly to the side, Katy gave him a look. "You're ridiculous, you know that? Gorillas don't know how to knit blankets."

His shoulders shook with silent laughter and he opened his mouth to no doubt offer another witty gorilla rejoinder but she was already back to scanning the sky. She held up her hand and pointed, drawing his attention to another cloud. "Look, what do you think that one is?"

Katy thought it looked like a turtle with a flower in its mouth or maybe a hunchbacked dragon, but she waited in silence for him to study it a bit, giving him time to draw his own conclusions.

"Beautiful," he finally said, but his voice had changed, dropping an octave—or maybe two. It was suddenly so low and husky and pensive Katy turned her head to stare at him in wonder, only to discover he was no longer looking at the clouds but he'd propped himself on his elbow again and was staring directly down at her.

Her breathing slowed and her heart skipped a beat.

Oh, no.

This could be trouble, she later remembered thinking, because he was staring down at her with such wistful yearning in his eyes. Whatever had been in her head after that was fuzzy; her thoughts became distorted and then silenced completely in reaction to the magic of their kiss.

In an instant, she was transported back to a time when nothing else mattered but the two of them. Her fingers reached out, threading themselves into his dark hair and as his head came down, his lips meeting and then fusing hungrily with hers, she could no longer hold open her eyes.

Matthew smelled of sweet memory and man and the comforting solace of homecoming. He tasted of summer frolic and happy laughter and the liquescent caress of sunshine and Katy could not deny herself the full pleasure of drinking him in.

Behind closed eyelids sun-dappled with shadow, imagery faded into intensity, became focused sensation and their separate existences were suddenly inexplicably entwined. Previously unspoken words of regrettably lost love and longing whispered out, though unintelligibly, on broken and breathy sighs.

Katy knew she was lost—*so* lost—and she was sinking; slowly and happily, she was eagerly drowning in a place to which she never should have come. In this place, Matthew was her only salvation, her only hope for survival and she held him close. Kissed him deeply. Clung to him for dear life. In his arms, her confusion and uncertainty melted away, erased by the promise he both made and shared in his kiss. She found herself lulled, lured in like a curious forest sprite to the light, into a trap of her own making.

Uncaring, unthinking, Katy kissed him for all she was worth, for old times' sake and for nothing more than the moment, greedily drinking in the sustaining breath of life that could only be Matthew while stubbornly ignoring the still, quiet warning in some distant, faraway place in the back of her mind that soon she would have to surface from this dream and go back to her normal life. And yet ...

Something was wrong.

Something felt suddenly terribly wrong and her intuitive knowing was what finally brought Katy out of the moment. Blinking, she opened her eyes. The sun glinted off the diamond in her engagement ring and she froze, her heart skipping a beat as her passions faded, leaving her feeling as if she'd just been plunged head first into a torrential river of ice.

Instantly, awareness of her surroundings returned. She was lying beneath the sun on a blanket with Matthew—*not* her *fiancé*—and they were both well on their way to being naked. Her shirt was tangled in Matthew's fingers and had been pushed up to her neck. His shirt was completely discarded and ...

Oh God, what have I done?

Katy's thoughts flew and her mind whirled as she fought to find footing in the dangerously eddying current of passion and emotion and regret that threatened to sweep her away, desperately groping her way through the mental and physical chaos to the shore.

Engaged to one man and kissing another had been one thing and she'd thought it could be reasonably excusable under the circumstances. But being engaged and making love to another man—even she knew that was totally and completely unacceptable.

Shameful.

Swallowing hard, she whispered a quick word of thanks that she'd realized what was about to happen and put a stop to it before things fully progressed.

With one palm pressing against Matthew's now bare shoulder while her other hand tugged down the hem of her blouse, Katy pushed him away, dislodging his tanned fingers in the process, and sat up before things really got out of hand.

Ignoring his disappointed groan of protest, she hurriedly scrambled to her feet to stare down at him, eyes blazing. "This is wrong, Matthew. *So* wrong. I'm *engaged.* I'm engaged and I know it, just like I knew I should never have come here today."

Straightening her shirt after leaning down to snatch up her purse from the side of the quilt where they had lain, she closed her eyes and covered them with a hand to her brow, finishing her conversation quietly but she knew Matthew heard every word. "I'm going to be *married* soon—to another man, and I—*oooh*, I just have to *go.*"

"Katy, hold on. Wait—"

Matthew reached out to her, but she shook her head almost violently and snatched her arm out of his reach. "No! No, don't try to fix this. Don't you *dare* try to fix this. And don't *say any*thing, Matthew. How could I? How could you? Oh God, how could *we*?"

Her gaze flitted unseeing around the clearing and she hopped on one foot while slipping her sandal onto the other. "This is not *me*. I am not this—this girl, this *woman* who—who promises herself to one man and gives herself to another. I *know* what a promise is, Matthew, and when I make one I keep it. I—I'm just ... not *like* this. Do you understand?"

Her eyes stung with tears of shame and confusion and she sucked in a breath to force them away while forcing her other foot into her other sandal. Footwear in place, she glared at him, her chest heaving with half-stifled sobs. "Don't call me again, Matthew. Don't call, don't come to see me, don't—don't do anything. Please, just ... nothing. Not anymore."

Anguish ripped through her at hearing the words she'd uttered. Words that basically tore him completely from her life. A nauseating wave of regret made her heart ache and the tears she'd been trying to hold back finally spilled over.

Matthew's expression changed immediately. His gaze shuttered but not before she saw the raw pain her words had caused him. Squeezing her eyes tight to block out the sight of his reaction, she said, "I'd hoped—I'd wanted us still to be friends but I can't. I can't do this, Matthew. Not with you."

Her eyes flashed open again allowing her misery-filled, watery gaze to search his in a desperate appeal for understanding.

Her plea reflected in his eyes, the desperate yearning in his gaze mirroring her own, but Matthew's silent regard urged her not to go while at the same time requesting something else entirely. Something different. Something more. Something she could no longer give. Not now. Not ever again.

Katy understood every aching, unspoken plea in his eyes but she could not disregard her promise, the promise she had made to marry another man. Finally, she whispered, "I'm sorry. I just *can't*."

MATTHEW BIT back a curse of utter frustration as he watched Katy scramble blindly through the trees to her car. She was hurting and he didn't like it at all but at the moment there was nothing he could do about it. Thinking—rational thinking, on Katy's part—was the only thing that could help her with this new pain.

He wanted to be angry with her for trying to cut him

out of her life with her words. With Ethan, too, for suggesting he take Katy on a trip down memory lane. As it turned out, although the trip was a bit misguided, he was happy because the resulting discovery he made was encouragingly the same: Katy still wanted him.

Sure, he got why she'd called a halt to their kissing. He was pretty sure he even knew why she'd left. Not that she would admit it—at least not to him, she was angry and confused and upset over what had happened between them because she hadn't expected things to go the way they had at all. She'd completely lost control of her desires and inside she felt ashamed.

Ashamed for wanting him, for not really being in love with her fiancé—and he thought that maybe he should feel a bit of shame, too, but he didn't because he was secretly thrilled with everything that had happened. Now he felt like he really had chance to win her back and damned if it didn't feel great!

The frustrating part, the bit Katy didn't seem to want to admit, was that this time it wasn't his fault. She'd been the one to reach for him and though he'd known he should at least have offered a show of resistance in light of her engagement announcement, he could not seem to find either the will or the strength to make himself turn her away.

Katy still wanted him and now they both knew she did. She could neither deny it, nor place the blame for her desire on him, no matter how desperately she might wish she could spin it another way. It was *her* yearnings, *her* passion and hunger that had made her reach out to him and he was happy with that—even if she had walked away in the end.

In an instant, his frustrations completely melted away and no matter how hard he tried, he couldn't keep himself from grinning. Katy still wanted him! And if she still wanted him, she might also still love him—or at least come to love him again.

Lying back on the blanket with renewed hope burning inside, Matthew tucked his hands behind his head and stared up at a perfect blue sky, his mind filled with possibilities and ideas as he planned what he would do to win back Katy's love.

One slow step at a time, he would remind her what it had been like for them before. He would reawaken her desire, not only for him, but for this place, Vine Falls—her *home*—which was where she really belonged. Maybe Katy had forgotten, but *he* hadn't. He would show her that this was where she was meant to be—not just for him but for her, too.

Katy belonged with people who really loved her, not with some guy who was too busy pimping his own worth to realize he was treating her like nothing more than an accessory, a bright, shiny object meant to be taken out and shone off only when other people were around to incite envy.

Oh, yes, he decided, Katy definitely needed to be reminded what it was like to live in this little rinky-dink speck of a town. Now if only he could figure out how to draw the wounded hellcat from her cave ...

CHAPTER 13

"Tell me again why we are getting married?" Katy asked Tipton when he called the next day after barely a few minutes into their conversation. She so needed to hear him to explain it, to tell her in his own words why he had asked her to be his wife.

She needed him to reassure her she was doing the right thing but she wanted him to do so by telling her all the gushy and romantic and yet completely believable little things she knew Matthew would say. The difference was, with Matthew she already knew every word he might say would be true.

For some reason, she held her breath while waiting for Tipton's reply. She wanted him to tell her they were getting married because he loved her, because he could not imagine living his life without her, but she also felt ashamed because her heart was doing a weird, jiggly little up and down dance in her chest. Not because she'd anticipated Tipton saying those wonderful things to her but because she'd slipped into her thoughts again and had been imagining it was Matthew on the other end of the call, teasing her, telling her why she belonged only to him and why the two of them were destined to be together forever.

Guilt over her afternoon frolic with Matthew had torn at her conscience long into the night and for most of the afternoon. Like a giddy teenager after a kiss by her first crush, Katy could not seem to stop herself from reliving the moment over and over again, which only made matters worse. By the time Tipton's call came through, she had beat herself up so many times over her mental affectionate defection, she ought to be black and blue.

The snarky little voice in her head snorted in disgust at the uselessness of her having hoped for such impractical, heart-felt answers from a man who thought attending a business banquet was equivalent to a romantic date.

Katy quickly shushed it, breathlessly waiting for Tipton's reply. After these past days with her old friends and most especially after the afternoon she'd spent with Matthew that had stirred up so much doubt in her mind, she'd really had to ask.

Her fears that she was marrying him for a heap of all

the wrong reasons and not a single one of the right ones had been tearing her up for days. She needed reaffirmation from him that he truly did care for her; that she wasn't making a mistake. But most of all she just needed to hear him say he loved her.

He could have ended her torment then and there, making every other thing in her life simple from that point forward but her hopeful anticipation collapsed, deflating like a pin-pricked balloon when his put-out sigh signaled the long-suffering lecture to come. His voice even managed to sound hopelessly tired when he asked, "Must we go through this again, Kate?"

Disappointed by his avoidance of her needs, and hearing him actually say he loved her was genuinely important to her, Katy's heart fell. But just as it had so many times before although she'd paid no attention at the time, her brain immediately began to supply reasons why it was okay if he didn't mention love. A man's need of a woman's presence on his arm was still a need for her to be in his life and that was good enough. Wasn't it?

"A man in my position requires a beautiful, intelligent woman like you in his life for many reasons, Kate, one of which is to act as hostess—an obligation I will be forced to hire an outsider to fill for the gala intro if you insist on staying down there indefinitely," he pointed out, inexplicably making her feel guilty for spending time with her family and friends.

He obviously would not say he loved her. In fact, she couldn't recall a time when he had ever said those words. How could she have been so blind? Maybe Matthew had been right. Maybe Tipton was only using her to make himself look desirable to others. Was she really prepared to give up the rest of her life to a man who would use her like that?

Tipton's voice droned on in her ear, but Katy had tuned him out, suddenly afraid Tipton's shunning any mention of a truly emotional attachment to her was proof that Matthew knew her *fiancé* better than she did.

※

LATER THAT NIGHT, Katy sat at a table at the Horseshoe with her friends, pretending to be celebrating. Although pride kept her back straight and her head up and her lips were smiling, inside she still wanted to cry. Her *fiancé* did not love her and she had only herself to blame for driving the one man who once had out of her life. She felt used on the one hand and utterly heartbroken on the other and she had never felt so alone in her life.

If only Matthew were here...

Looking around at the empty tables beside them—it was Wednesday night, after all—she suddenly wished they were crammed with her old friends and acquaintances, that she could go back in time to a day when her life—her future—was not so complicated and she was not so on the verge of giving in to a good squall.

Before she could work herself up to full-on depression, LoraLynn whistled for attention as she held up a pair of icy cold drinks Gin had brought over form the bar which she plunked down in front of Katy.

"Katy Ann Wallace, these suds are for you—and this is is your *official* welcome home to Vine Falls!" she offered with a big grin and Katy had to remind herself they were supposed to be celebrating. She was the guest of honor and as such duty bound to enjoy herself, so she forced herself to raise the glass.

"Here's to small towns and the company of good friends," she called out and then made a hooting sort of cheering noise before taking a hearty swallow.

Amber was the first to follow suit. "I'll drink to that!"

"Here, here!" Sadie offered, lifting her own glass.

"Woo-hoo!" LoraLynn cheered and lifted her drink in salute, but Katy noticed she didn't actually sip from it at all. Her brow furrowed for a moment in confusion as she tried to puzzle out why but the answer, like the ones she'd been seeking to her personal dilemmas, refused to present itself and Katy pushed her curiosity away. Tonight was supposed to be a party, she reminded herself, and now was not the time for probing questions.

Surrounded by all her girlfriends at the Horseshoe for what LoraLynn had deemed a welcome home party,

Katy lifted the celebratory mug and took another long swallow before reminding them she soon would be leaving again. It was true. She had to go back—she had a wedding to plan even if she was suddenly thinking it was a pity she couldn't stay here forever.

"Oh, that's right. Katy here's about to get married and we've never met the man! What kind of hometown girl gets herself engaged without letting her best friends vet her boyfriend?" Amber asked, leaning back and sort of sideways in her chair as she pretended to glare across the table at Katy. "Come on, Katy. We can't get to him, so it's all up to you now. You've got to tell us about your fiancé."

With her forefinger, Katy pushed her glasses high, resettling them more comfortably onto the bridge of her nose. She had known this moment would eventually come but hadn't realized how unsettling it would be. Before, she had envisioned a gushing, glowing spiel as she told her friends about the man she was marrying. Only now she no longer thought of Tipton the same way.

Still, she had to say something. Her friends were all waiting for her to tell them about this wonderful man she had met when she'd left home. But telling them about Tipton when all she could think of was Matthew was going to be a bit difficult.

"Well, you all know his name already, right? Tipton Van Warner the Third. He's twenty-nine years old and while I wouldn't say he is devastatingly handsome, I think he's able to hold his own."

Sadie rolled her eyes and grinned. "Like you would fall for an ugly man."

Once again her thoughts went immediately to Matthew. No, he was not ugly at all and never had been. Even in middle school he'd been the best looking guy in her class and by the time high school ended, he'd become one fine specimen of a man. Shifting again in her chair to hide her shiver of delight, Katy decided Sadie was absolutely right—Matthew could never be classed as ugly.

"What does he look like? Is he tall? Broad in the shoulder? Come on, Katy, you've got to tell it all!"

Katy blinked in momentary confusion. Were they asking about Matthew or Tipton? The answer, she realized, was Tipton. Duh. This was no time to be confused. An embarrassed half-laugh and bit of a shy smile were taken for hesitant abashment—her friends would think she was reluctant to tell them how gorgeous her fiancé was and Katy secretly wished it were true.

She wished it were true almost as much as she wished she could feel as eager about her *fiancé* and her upcoming wedding as a woman in love ought to feel. *Should* feel. As a soon-to-be-bride, blast it, she had every right. But discussing her groom over drinks with her friends, Katy didn't feel anywhere near excited.

In fact, ever since her phone call with Tipton this

afternoon, she had felt downright depressed to be marrying him. Not that she could tell her friends about it. They expected a happy bride to be and her pride said she must give it to them. Shifting in her chair, she injected a bit of false delight and just a bit of awe into her tone, hoping it would pass for sincerity.

"Tipton's not as tall as Ethan or Matthew but he's not short like BobbyJoe, either," she winked at LoraLynn to let her know she was kidding. "He has light brown hair that's kind of curly and it comes down just below his shoulders. He wears glasses, though his are wire rimmed instead of gawky and black like mine, and he's fond of designer business suits."

"Oh, now I have an image of that guy from that frontier show Mama always used to watch—he was the bratty spoiled blond girl's fiancé. What was his name?" She snapped her fingers as if it would help her to remember.

"We don't care, Amber. We want to know more about Katy's guy, not delve into TV trivia," Sadie said with a roll of her eyes, then motioned for Katy to continue.

"He works for a brokerage. It's a highly respected firm," she assured them. "Hubaker, Mailer, and Skye? He's also into politics—he is already a junior councilman and has high hopes of being mayor someday."

"A money man, huh? Ooh, already I can tell he's going to be a real genuine guy," Amber teased with a roll of her eyes which said she expected no such thing. LoraLynn gave her a friendly smack on the shoulder with an admonishment to stop it and Katy thought of Matthew.

If he had been with them tonight, he would have poked fun at her fiancé, just like Amber. Only she would have taken offense had the slight come from him. Why didn't it bother her so much coming from Amber? *Because you know she's right*, came the voice in her head, *and you aren't trying to hide your real feelings from her the way you do with Matthew.*

Katy knew it was true. It was okay for Amber to say what she thought because unlike with herself and Matthew when they talked about Tipton, she wasn't constantly comparing the two.

"So, a broker who's into politics, huh? A little odd maybe, or maybe not." Amber shrugged at the unusual combination. "I just can't figure out for the life of me how the two of you got together. Was it fate? Love at first sight and all that jazz? Or did you somehow just bumble into each other?"

Katy took a sip of her drink to hide her snort and almost choked instead. Wiping at the beer foam mustache with her fingers, she took a deep breath and blinked a few times before she got herself under control and then she shook her head. "Actually it was more a matter of necessity."

Amber's left brow rose. "That sounds ominous and now you have to spill. Tell us, where did you meet him, how did you meet him, and were you alone when you met or did you have someone with you?"

She'd ticked each item off on her fingers and Katy was reminded of one of those TV shows where the casual acquaintance was actually wired and seeking the truth for some hidden investigator. How much of the desperation she'd felt at the time did she want to reveal here?

"I wasn't alone because I was working—no, you don't even want to know where. He needed a hostess, I needed a job. Tipton took one look at me and decided I fit the part admirably. Things just kind of progressed from there," Katy admitted, even though it hurt how depressing it felt because how she'd met her future husband was as far from being cute and romantic as could be humanly possible.

"I guess his need for a hostess explains the clothes, the posh hair style, and the sophisticated new Katy Wallace we all caught a glimpse of when you rolled back into town," Amber surmised.

Katy thought it just proved Tipton had wanted a dress up doll and she'd been naive enough to fall for the job, but Amber wasn't finished. "And by the size of that rock on your finger, I'd say his proposal came as a nice little promotion."

Katy glanced at her engagement ring, thinking Matthew would get a kick out of that: a promotion. An ornament for an ornament and a pretty he could show off to all his friends and business partners—that's what her engagement to Tipton had really been.

That exact moment was finally when Katy realized her relationship with Tipton Van Warner was a lot less about love and romance than it was about how he looked to the public eye. With Tipton, it was all about his business position.

The only real love she'd ever had came from Matthew—and she'd pretty much killed that by leaving before he proposed and then showing up years later with a fiancé to hurt him all over again. Blinking back tears she tried to cover with a fake watery smile, Katy nodded and made a noise of agreement. "It's nice—comes with lots of little perks. A car. Designer clothes. Designer shoes. Lots more jewelry—"

Sadie snorted. "Hey, with all that on offer for a wife maybe I should marry him, too."

CHAPTER 14

It was after midnight and the rest of the girls had already gone home—they all had to work tomorrow—LoraLynn did too, but she had stayed to help Gin clean up and so, supposedly, had Katy.

Only sometime between the last call and lock up, Katy had fallen into a bit of a drunken slumber.

Leaning close, LoraLynn shook her by the shoulder to hopefully jostle her back to awareness. "Katy? Katy, wake up, hon, and give me your keys. I'm going to have to call someone to drive you home."

Katy had her head down on her arms lying on the table in front of her. She was snoring and her mouth was slack and LoraLynn was tempted to snap a picture with her phone. She wasn't sure how it had happened because she hadn't really been paying that much attention to the drinks, but Katy had gotten herself worse than drunk—she was totally sloshed. That was a bit beyond inebriated. Unable to stand, much less swing a broom, Katy was a really serious mess. LoraLynn shook her head and turned to Gin to confess. "I think this is the first time I've ever seen her this way."

To Katy, she asked, "How many drinks did you have, anyway?"

Katy slowly lifted her head, making a slurping noise as she did so before making a half-hearted sleep-weary swipe at the drool smeared on her cheek and chin. "Not jure. I slopped counting astfer three and Matthew's gonna be mad. He shays I'm not a wery—a very good drun—he's—I'm never a berry good drinker."

Lifting her head a bit more, Katy squinted, peering up at her through bleary eyes. "Hey, you're the pershon who's 'ponsible for throwin' tonight's party to begin with so you don't nudge—don't judge me and I don't even have a home here, LoraLynn. I'm staying with my mother down on schickty-eight a ways, remember?"

"If I can't find your keys in this thing, for tonight at least, you'll be staying in a bar," LoraLynn muttered around an amused grin before she finally found Katy's purse—it was tucked under the coat she had been half lying and half sitting on.

By the time she located the keys, Katy was trying to

get to her feet by herself and making very little progress before giving up and slowly shaking her head.

"Oh, no. I can't! I can't schtay in a bar. What would Mrs. Van Wormer—no, Van *Warner* think of her schoon to be laughter-in-daw then?" Leaning to one side, she attempted to whisper, "I'm no good for her shon, LoraLynn."

"Oh, I'm sure she loves you, sweetie," LoraLynn said while fishing out her cell phone. She decided it would probably be easier to call BobbyJoe and have him get Ethan to drive him over to pick up the car. She would drive Katy home herself, and BobbyJoe could stop by there to get her.

"Nope," Katy insisted while she waited for BobbyJoe to answer her call. "I'm a scheat and a—a scheat and a schlowlife boozher."

She dropped down suddenly, falling back into the chair with her hands hanging loosely at her sides. Turning unexpectedly tear-filled eyes upward, she asked LoraLynn, "How could I make love with him when I's—I'm enraged to another man?"

LoraLynn moved to stand in front of her to keep her in the chair until she could gather up their things. Katy wrapped her arms around LoraLynn's middle, laid her head on her stomach and tearfully asked, "Why can't he ever enen jus' be who I wan—who I want him to be?"

Who is she talking about? Gin mouthed from across

the table. LoraLynn's brow rose high but she only shrugged in answer.

"You mean Tipton?" she guessed, all the while hooking both her purse and Katy's over her shoulder. "I'm sure he's really a wonderful man, Katy, but we don't want him to see you like this, do we?"

BobbyJoe finally answered and after a quick explanation, she shoved her cell phone into her purse and heaved a resigned sigh. "I don't know exactly how I'm going to manage this, Gin, but I promise I am going to get her out of here before morning."

Shifting to get her shoulder under one of Katy's arms, LoraLynn stood up again, straightening as best she could under Katy's dragging weight and motioned for Gin to hold open the door. To Katy, she said, "Come on, sweetie. Let's get you to the car."

They'd moved about three steps when Katy suddenly lifted her head and gave an exaggerated nod. "Tistfton, yesh. Tha's who I mean. Why can't he jus' be Matthew? Although that would be kind of baszhar, wooden it? If Tishton were—if Tipston was ashaley Mashew?"

Her sudden frown was highly exaggerated by her inebriated state and LoraLynn couldn't help but smile a little until she finished with, "But then I couldn't sit on his car!"

Katy started to giggle, and that giggle soon became a fit of laughter she couldn't seem to contain. Still busily trying to hold on to Katy and struggling beneath her rag doll weight to keep them both upright, LoraLynn bit back a grin. It was already hard to keep them both on their feet with all the shaking, stumbling, and falling around she was doing, and then Katy kept on laughing. She laughed until the sound of it became contagious and then LoraLynn was laughing with her, too. Even Gin couldn't contain her smile.

"Let me help you get her to the car," Gin offered after a bit, and having finally tamed the unstoppable belly laughs down to an involuntarily recurring chuckle, LoraLynn managed a nod.

"It's those steps outside I'm really worried about. Can you get in front of us so between the two of us we can make sure she doesn't tip over and fall on her face?"

"I did awready that, LiriaLynn. I left an' I fell. I fell right on my fashe and—but none of it worked," Katy slurred before her chin drooped down, her expression the epitome of sadness. "I'm still nothin' more better than a schatistik."

"Whatever that means," Gin muttered quietly. When Katy said nothing else, she nodded her head at LoraLynn. "I'm ready when you are."

Tightening her hold on Katy's all but limp arm, Lora-Lynn nodded. "We'll go on the count of three."

By the time they managed to get Katy stabilized and in the passenger side seat of her car, LoraLynn was exhausted. Leaning over to buckle Katy's seat belt on, she straightened suddenly and waved her hand in front of her face. "Whoa, booze breath. Gin, will you dig in the side of my purse for my tic-tacs? I think she's going to need a handful."

Gin snickered at that but did as she was asked. "Here ya go. You two going to be alright?"

LoraLynn closed the door and leaned heavily against it. "Yeah, I think so, if I can get her inside the house once I get her home. You sure you don't mind waiting here for BobbyJoe?"

Gin waved her concern away. "It's fine. Probably won't be more than five minutes after you leave. I'll give him your keys, then lock up and go home."

Rounding the back of the car, LoraLynn opened the driver's door and tossed her purse inside. "Thanks, Gin, and thanks again for letting us come in on an off-night."

As she drove to the Wallace place, Katy woke up off and on, each time mumbling about her fiancé and Matthew and how everything with both of the men in her life was bad and had gone drastically, terribly wrong. LoraLynn bit her tongue and didn't ask any of the leading questions she wanted to ask but she had a feeling when morning came around Katy would be calling with a few of her own.

To her welcome surprise, Matthew was waiting for them when she pulled into the drive at the Wallace place

—BobbyJoe had called ahead and given him a heads-up, he said. He was supposed to pick up LoraLynn and drop her off at home, but she was hoping he'd help her get Katy awake and out of the car again so she could make sure she made up to the house and then managed to get herself safely inside.

"I'll take her in if you want," he offered, and at that point LoraLynn didn't even care if Katy might get upset. She was her friend, but she was exhausted and more than ready to go home. Handing him Katy's purse, she nodded and he effortlessly scooped Katy into his arms.

LoraLynn followed them to the house, pressing one hand against the aching small of her back. She unlocked the front door and Matthew carried Katy up the stairs to her old room as quietly as he could manage while LoraLynn opened the door and straightened the bed before putting away her coat and purse. He laid Katy on the bed and took off her shoes, then leaned down to brush a tangle of hair off her face.

In her drunken slumber, Katy murmured his name and something else and LoraLynn noticed Matthew couldn't help but smile. Unwilling to intrude on what might quickly become a personal moment, LoraLynn ducked her head and walked out into the hallway to wait for him outside.

He followed almost immediately but she couldn't help but overhear what he'd whispered right before he sighed and stepped away from the bed to follow her on out. He'd said, "I'll always love you, fairy girl," and Lora-Lynn thought it might have been Matthew's way of saying goodbye. But there had been such a wealth of emotion in both his tone and in his sigh—the soul deep sadness and longing she'd heard there almost made her cry.

KATY WAS DREAMING.

She knew she was dreaming because in her dream Matthew was standing over her, his fingers tenderly brushing the hair away from her face while he whispered something to her, but she felt woozy and everything was kind of a blur.

Rolling over onto her back, she blinked, trying to focus in the dark room, to hear what he was saying, but he had already disappeared. She wasn't sure which bothered her more: his disappearance or the fact that she hadn't quite heard whatever he'd said to her, but whichever it was, she was now wide awake.

Staring blindly up at the textured ceiling, bits of memory from her last few minutes at her "welcome home party" drifted into her immediate recall. She knew she ought to feel horrible about some of the things she'd said, be embarrassed about what she had revealed if

LoraLynn had been paying close enough attention to piece things together, but right now she was too hurt and depressed by the revelation she'd had to care.

Her *fiancé* did not love her.

The man she had come here to tell everyone about, the man she was supposed to go back to in less than a week and then marry soon after only cared about how stable, secure, and lucky her being by his side made him look to his associates.

He didn't care about her.

He only cared that he wasn't forced to pay an outside service to host his private schmooze parties or that he wasn't bothered to go through the trouble of putting forth the effort to have a real relationship. Tipton had asked her to marry him when what he'd really wanted was an assistant, not a bride.

He didn't want her in his life at all—at least not in the capacity she needed to be wanted.

How could she have been so blind? Being so caught up in her own need to change things, to have a different life than the one she'd always known and to be something more, something better, she supposed she'd only seen what she wanted to see.

Maybe that was why she'd felt such a strong urge to get away from it all for a few weeks, to come back to Vine Falls where life was infinitely more quiet, more relaxed and settled? She supposed she'd simply needed the distance—from both Tipton and the lifestyle into which she had allowed him to lead her—to be able to look back and see what was missing from their relationship.

And tonight she had seen all to clearly that what was missing was friendship. Caring. Love.

It would be kind of hard for anyone to see more clearly than she did now that marrying Tipton would be a colossal mistake. But seeing with absolute clarity didn't make the momentous discovery hurt any less.

And then there was Matthew...

Wonderful, amazing, sensitive, beautiful Matthew who had loved her once. He had wanted to marry her, too, to share his life with her in a way she wasn't sure Tipton would even recognize. How many times during those years before she'd gone away had Matthew looked her in the eyes and foolishly promised her the world? Too many, she recalled, huffing out a sigh.

Katy knew he'd believed he would somehow find a way to give it to her, too, or make a way himself if he must. *She* had been the one filled with hesitance and doubt, and she had also been the one who'd ruined whatever chance she might have had at finding happiness with him four years ago. Then, a couple weeks ago, she had come home to flout her engagement and ended up underestimating her own self control and foolishly poked the bear that was her own inability to resist loving him when he was near.

Still, Matthew had wanted to be friends. He was the one who had extended the olive branch. He was the one who had made the effort to bring her back into his life, albeit in the role of friendship this time, but she had lost control and completely destroyed whatever might have come of that effort, too.

Thinking back to the picnic and all the things she'd said to him after they'd kissed, after they had almost made love right there in the same clearing from which she had fled once before, she knew the bridges that might have been mended to close the distance four years of being apart had created between them had been burned.

How he must hate her now.

Twice burned, twice spurned by the same woman, Matthew probably never wanted to see her again, and truly, she could not blame him. If their situations were reversed, she would feel the same.

The problem was that she still loved him.

Only now, admitting it to either herself or to Matthew wouldn't do either of them any good.

Whatever might once have been between them now was gone. She had killed it, if not before then certainly when she had walked into the Horseshoe with Tipton last night, and had no one to blame but herself.

Rolling onto her side, Katy hugged her pillow close and let her silent tears seep into the flowery cotton pillow slip. She would have to go back to face Tipton. Even if he didn't deserve it, she would call off their wedding in person, face-to-face.

And after that? She wasn't sure. Not yet. But she did know she had some big decisions to make over the next few days. Her return flight was scheduled for Monday, which meant she had four days to come to terms with everything she had discovered tonight and then decide what she was going to do with the next phase of her life.

CHAPTER 15

Matthew had been looking forward to tonight since Katy had left him at the picnic on Wednesday so there was no wonder his brother caught him in a better mood while he was getting ready to go out. Poking his head around the open bathroom door, Liam gave him an odd look.

"You're whistling," he needlessly pointed out. "Got a hot date?"

A hot date. Yeah, he would say Katy more than qualified as hot. As for the date part... well, all he knew for sure was that for the first time in four years he was actually looking forward to joining his friends at the Horseshoe.

"Just going down to the Horseshoe with friends, like

I do every Friday night," he hedged, not wanting to let his little brother see how important tonight really was to him. Despite their little argument on Wednesday, he felt sure Katy would be there and he could hardly wait to see her again. To talk with her and dance with her. To experience the pleasure of just having her by his side.

Tonight he planned do and say everything he could to remind Katy of all the things she'd once loved about him and home, to help her recall how perfect life had been between them four years ago. And he figured wearing a splash or two of her favorite cologne couldn't hurt matters none, so he upended the bottle in his hand and gave his face a couple of pats.

Liam wrinkled his nose. "Wow, Matthew. Now you smell worse than the girls bathroom at school."

"Hey, wait till you're older and you'll be scenting yourself up, too." He grinned. "The ladies love this stuff."

Figuring Liam was done trying to torture him with younger sibling banter for the minute, Matthew put his shaving equipment away and reached to pull his clean t-shirt over his head. As soon as it cleared his eyes, he noticed his brother still standing there, watching him with a puzzled expression. "What?"

Liam shrugged. "You're different. Almost like you were before. Is that 'cause Katy's back?"

Matthew felt funny discussing his past and his love

life with his kid brother and his discomfort must have showed on his face because Liam shrugged and leaned against the door frame to explain.

"Some of the kids at school mentioned some of the old coots at church were talking about it and wondering if the two of you were going to finally patch things up. They were wondering if you and Katy were going to get back together. Are you?"

It's too soon to tell, Matthew wanted to say, but there were too many other hurdles standing in the way.

When he didn't answer right away, Liam filled the silence with another tidbit of overheard gossip. "I also heard she's engaged, that she came home to tell her mother about the wedding. I guess that's why she hasn't dropped in to say hi to Mom and me."

That much Matthew knew was true, so he nodded, but Liam still had questions it seemed.

"You gonna break it up? The engagement, I mean." He shrugged and kicked at the bottom of the door frame with his tennis shoe encased heel before peering up at Matthew again. "If you still love her and y'all are gonna get back together, you're kinda sorta gonna have to, aren't you?"

Matthew stifled a curse and bit back a groan. This was where he had to explain to his brother that it wasn't right to go messing around in other people's lives, that good guys didn't go around trying to steal other men's women away from them when he knew that was exactly what he intended to try and do.

In the few seconds between Liam's question and his answer, Matthew tried to figure out if him getting between Katy and her future husband would be okay since he had loved Katy first, but before he could even finish the thought he already knew the answer.

"No. No, Liam, I'm not going to try and get Katy to break her engagement. I do want her to remember how good things once were between us and what life was like with me but in the end," he shrugged. "The decision is entirely up to her."

Liam shook his head, clearly not impressed by his answer. "You really are an idiot, man. You ain't even gonna stand up and fight for her? If it was my girl and I wanted her back, I'd be dropping down on some nose."

He mimicked the kind of elbow drop he would use and Matthew had to pretend it wasn't a move he'd already thought of making on Katy's absent fiancé a time or two himself. Still, he frowned down at his little brother—the last thing he wanted to encourage was Liam fighting some guy over a girl. "Fighting doesn't solve anything, Liam. You know it only makes matters worse."

Liam nodded and kicked the door frame with his heel again. "Yeah, sorry. I didn't mean to bring you down again. That's actually what I interrupted your shave to tell you in the first place."

Matthew was lost. "That you didn't want to bring me down again?"

Liam made a face and shook his head. "No, dork. The other bit. The part where you were acting like you used to before."

"Ah, that." Matthew nodded, indicating he'd got it but now Liam was looking down the hall toward the stairs as if he were embarrassed to meet Matthew's gaze.

Finally, his tone between teasing and one hundred percent serious, he admitted, "I kind of like you when you're whistling and reeking of stinky cologne and in a girl-struck kind of daze."

"Yeah?" Matthew asked as he picked up his towel and aimed it at the hamper for dirty clothes. He missed; the towel landed in a damp mound beside it, and Liam boo-ed his terrible aim while Matthew only shrugged then grinned as he reached out to ruffle Liam's hair, pushing past him and into the hallway before he made his way to his room. "You know, Liam, maybe I should mention my change of behavior to Katy tonight when I see her because I kind of like me better this way, too."

Liam snorted and after another wrinkle of his nose, he pulled the neck of his shirt up until it almost covered his eyes and said, "I dunno. Whatever, man. If you think it would help, do what you gotta do—but first you need to get rid of that stinky man perfume."

※

Upstairs in her old room again, Katy gave herself a quick misting of her favorite perfume then leaned close to the full-length mirror to slide on a light layer of lip gloss. That done, she stood back, inspecting herself with a critical eye as she got ready for what she suspected would be her last visit ever to the Horseshoe in Vine Falls.

She had already pulled on a pair of faded denim jeans and a loose t-shirt, relics from the closet of her youth which surprisingly still fit—or was it that they fit again?—but she had a nagging feeling something was still missing. Her gaze drifted down her body to her bare toes scrunched deep in the carpet and she laughed. She'd definitely discovered what was missing: *shoes*.

Another trip to her dresser and then the closet turned up socks and then a pair of her old tennis shoes, which she quickly stuffed her now socked feet in. Back at the mirror, she turned this way and that, marveling at the effect a simple change of clothing style could have on a person's body but also their entire outlook on life.

On the outside, at least, she quickly amended. Other

than the lack of joy or excitement in her eyes and the tiny smattering of tell-tale lines revealing traces of her recent emotional strain near the edges of her lips, she almost looked eighteen again.

Would Matthew notice? She wondered, then pushed the hope that immediately flared in her gut into the darker recesses of her being. Tonight would not be about Matthew. Instead, this one last night of fun and frolic among lifelong friends would be solely about Katy Wallace.

Tonight, she'd decided, she would turn off the "other" Katy—the smart, chic, sophisticated lady who looked the part of a woman about to become the wife of a future public official. Tonight, she would simply be *herself*, the spontaneous, nature-and fun-loving girl she once had been a long time ago—the Katy Wallace both she and all her friends used to know and love.

It surprised her how much she was looking forward to it and how much her decision to let go of the new to embrace the old just somehow seemed to "fit," but right now her old life felt more comfortable to her than any other moment since she'd left here four years ago.

It was strange to think a simple decision had somehow changed her life overnight.

Downstairs, the doorbell pealed and her heart leaped; a thrill of giddy anticipation raced through her.

For some reason, she thought it might be Matthew coming to call despite her orders not to. "I've got it, Mama!" she hollered down the hall as she booked it from her room. She rushed down the stairs two at a time to snatch open the door, her lips curved in a ready smile. "Hello! Oh, I am so glad you cam—" Her voice caught and her smile faded. "Tipton. What are you doing here?"

"Were you expecting someone else?" His cool, narrow-eyed inspection wilted every petal of excitement that had been flowering inside her, replacing them with prickling thorns of irritation. Shifting from one foot to the other, she glanced toward the kitchen, wondering how rude it would be if she suddenly raced for freedom in the second biggest escape of her life, straight out through the back door.

"Expecting? No," she hedged while wondering what in the world he was doing here. She didn't mention she'd actually been *wishing* someone else would be there to greet her when she'd rushed wide open as a freight train down the stairs like a teenager. Nor did she admit she was doubly disappointed to open it and find her fiancé waiting for her instead, or how much she had secretly hoped Matthew would be the one waiting for her on the other side of that door.

Uncomfortable in what might as well have been the uniform of her youth under her fiancé's censorious gaze, she fidgeted, her fingers picking nervously at the doorknob while she fought the urge to rush back upstairs and change, but she couldn't just leave him standing there! Stepping back two steps, she offered a hesitant, apologetic smile and motioned toward the living room.

"Come inside, Tipton. Mama's upstairs. I'll just run up and let her know you've arrived."

CHAPTER 16

Katy was tense and on edge walking into the Horseshoe with Tipton by her side. Decked out in Armani from head to toe, he was too different from the jeans-clad, flannel-wearing regular Friday night crowd not to stick out among them like a sore thumb, but he'd refused to change although she'd more than hinted he ought to dress down some.

Silently mourning for at least the fifth time already the loss of a fun, relaxing evening with friends she had hoped to have, Katy cast a pitying eye at her soon-to-not-be *fiancé* and sighed. Tipton Van Warner would never understand the finer nuances of mingling in a southern small town night spot. Not the way she and rest of her friends did—the way anyone did who had lived here all their lives.

Not only that, she had a terrible feeling he wasn't going to rub along too well with her friends. It didn't take a psychic to see he obviously didn't belong here anymore than she had belonged anywhere with him in his high-class, hustle and hurry big city world, or even in his life at all.

Despite her desire earlier today to see Matthew here tonight, her most fervent wish at the moment was that this would be the one Friday night when he wouldn't bother to put in an appearance at all. It was not meant to be, however, because as soon as she walked through the front door of the Horseshoe, she saw him sitting in his usual spot at the back corner table—only tonight he wasn't wearing a scowl.

Sprawled with his legs outstretched in front of him, he lounged in his usual chair and he was looking straight at the door when she walked through behind Tipton. His easy smile slowly disappeared, and Katy stifled a groan because she knew there was just no way she could pretend she hadn't seen him. Pushing her discomfort and misgivings away and straightened her spine as she put her arm through Tipton's.

As casually as she could manage, she hitched her chin up a notch and marched determinedly forward. Still, her smile was more than a little wobbly when she reached Matthew's table and when he only sat there in silence and stared at her with a mixture of agony and haunting appeal in his eyes, her courage almost flew straight out the window.

Matthew stared up at her, one brow arched in question until she finally found her courage and her voice. "Tipton Van Warner, I would like you to meet Matthew Shaw. Matthew, this is Tipton, my—uhm, yeah, my *fiancé*."

Forcing a smile, he put out a hand after Katy made the introductions, thinking all the while there had to be some special reward for any man who could manage to sit calmly with his hands at his sides while another man casually touched the woman he should never have had a right to touch—in this case, the woman Matthew had always considered to be his own.

"Ah, so *this* is the elusive uhm-*fiancé*?" he teased in true past-Matthew fashion while through narrowed eyes he rudely inspected the guy from toe to top, mentally cataloging all the ways he was not the right man for Katy.

Forcing himself to keep his hand out in offer of an age-old gesture of acknowledgment, he squelched the protest screaming in his heart and head to say, "Welcome to Vine Falls, man."

The tight-lipped smile Tipton gave as he reached out to shake Matthew's hand was more smirking grimace than anything. Letting his arm drop, Matthew glanced between the two, his eyes lingering on Katy's a second more than it probably should have.

In that brief moment of time he felt a part of him break that hadn't yet broken before though there were no sparks to commemorate it. There was no crumbling expression, no tight smile. As far as outward appearances went, he showed absolutely nothing but he now knew quietly losing one's soul was far more painful than merely dying inside because letting Katy go for real was a helluva lot worse than he'd ever imagined it would be.

Catching Katy's gaze, Matthew smiled again, only this time the gesture was sadly genuine. He knew what she could see painfully reflected in the depths of his eyes because it was exactly what he wanted her to see: proof of his realization, that this time he got it. Whatever he might once have had with her was finally really over.

For four years, he'd hoped. After the picnic, he'd wanted and foolishly thought he might actually have a chance. Now he knew the truth: what once had been between them would never be so again and it was high time he acknowledged it; time he stopped trying to get back what obviously had never really been his. The past was built on memory for a reason, he reminded himself, and it was time he started treating it as such. Without another word spoken or unspoken to either of them, he slid back his chair, got to his feet, and headed for the door.

Outside, the cool night air rushed over him and he breathed it in deep, welcoming the biting crispness of it as it hit his lungs. In a sort of daze, he walked to his truck, started it up and pulled out of the lot and then onto the main road. For a long while, he drove in silence before finally turning on the radio, an act he immediately regretted because he was blasted by a doleful song that was all about might-have-been's.

His thoughts stuck on Katy and her *fiancé* and all that he had lost, Matthew started to turn it off. Hearing it would only make the numbness in his body dissipate and he sorely needed its presence right now—it was the only thing his current state of shock allowed him to feel and it was all he had to remind him he was still alive.

The numbness was about the only thing allowing him to remember how to function. But something in the words of the song—or maybe it was just the laid-back melody?—made him leave it alone. With nowhere to be and no particular place in mind that he cared to go, Matthew put his hand back on the wheel and just listened.

※

FROM OVER THE top of Tipton's head, Katy watched Matthew leave with the sting of tears in her eyes, wondering how he could be so casual about it all when she was quietly breaking in two inside. There had been no scene, no testosterone-laden man show, but there had definitely been a farewell in Matthew's eyes, in his silent departure—one only she would recognize. It was written in the careful way he'd walked across the room with his shoulders back and his head held high. Shadowed by the hastily buried pain in his eyes and way he'd slipped quietly out the door without bothering to say goodbye, and when the door closed behind him Katy knew then that the last chapter of the Katy and Matthew portion of the story of her life was now officially over.

She wanted so badly to run after him, to beg him to wait for her, to take her with him wherever he wanted to go. But there were things she'd needed to take care of first—and she knew it was already much too late.

Turning away, she shivered from the loss of his presence, cold now where only hours before she had been flushed and giddy with excitement, and suddenly realized it had always been that way for her with him. When Matthew was present, her world shined bright but when he left her, it was as if he'd taken everything good and right away with him, leaving her with an empty feeling and slightly chilled inside.

Tipton's brittle mockery of a smile was a cold token of unknowing condolence in light of what she had just lost. When she'd come back here three weeks ago, she'd thought she gotten exactly what she wanted, was sure she had found it all. Now? Now she knew true regret. Knew nothing in her life would ever be the same again.

But for this one last night, she decided amidst the chaos that was her pain, she was going to do her best to stand and smile until she somehow managed to finally muddle her way through it.

She was strong. She could handle one last night, even if it meant she had to to ignore the crushing pain in her heart, the slip in her smile to just take what the night had brought and try to make the best of it.

She didn't last an hour.

Confused by what she wished she could do and knowing all the while she needed to do something entirely different, Katy kept glancing at the door, desperately hoping Matthew would turn around, that he would decide to come back to her after all. But every time the door opened and she recognized yet another of her friends instead, her hope grew a little more dim.

Sadie and Jensen came through first, followed by LoraLynn and BobbyJoe. Ethan was already there but he hadn't yet come over to her and Tipton's table yet to say hello and she didn't think she was up to searching for him, either. Not that it mattered, she thought, spying Sadie and the others slowly making their way over. For the next few minutes at the very least, she was about to have company.

The next two hours were filled with chatter during which Katy was forced to deal with re-hearing the same old stories and jokes she'd already heard at least a million times before. Her friends were in true form, determined to make sure Tipton knew exactly what he was getting into by marrying their Katy. One by one, they each recounted to him the horror stories of her life.

Not only that, the guys pitched in to do their parts to make Tipton as uncomfortable as possible, purposely getting in digs on the city slicker—some of their jabs would actually have been beyond insulting if Tipton had realized what they meant. By the time the conversation wound down and the dancing started, Katy's nerves were completely worn thin.

It was barely ten when she decided enough was enough. She had to get out of there, and the sooner she did it the better it would be for everyone because if she had to force one more smile or deal with one more touch of Tipton's hand lingering on her arm where she knew Matthew's rightly should have been, she would surely shatter to her bones.

Pasting on a tight-lipped smile, she excused herself to go to the restroom. Once there, she locked the door and tiredly leaned against it, taking in deep breaths through her nose to try to quell the sudden nausea she felt rising to the fore.

Her eyes burned with inexplicable tears and she pressed the heels of both hands tight against them before shoving away from the door and hurrying to the sink where she flicked on the cold water and then splashed her face with it at least a few dozen times.

Once she was marginally sure she was no longer one wrong breath from shattering into pieces on the floor, she glanced up to look at her face in the mirror and was immediately horrified. The person who stared back at her was a complete stranger to her—she was no longer someone she knew. There was no light in her eyes, no color in her cheeks—it was like Matthew had taken with him her will to live when he'd walked out that door tonight.

She wanted to be angry at him for it, but knew she had no right to be. Everything that had happened from the minute she stepped foot back in Vine Falls had been her own fault, of her own making or otherwise her own doing but knowing didn't make the hurt any less painful to bear. Still staring at her reflection, she squinted at the girl locked within the glass and whispered, "Katy Wallace, what have you done?"

When she walked out a good five minutes later, Ethan was leaning against the wall outside the door. He had obviously been waiting for her because he straightened as she approached, cornering her for a private word before she could slip past him and go back to her table.

There was something in his eyes she only noticed when she was too close to ignore it, something that gave her pause and made her suddenly reluctant to speak with him. When he opened his mouth, she immediately knew why: he was fighting back a tightly controlled anger.

Not many knew it about him, but Katy was one of the few who did—Ethan Jones had a temper that meant bad news for anyone dumb enough to light his fuse—and tonight she was the dumb one it seemed. She also knew his temper was generally slow-burning, which meant whatever she had done, she must have set fire to it the minute she'd came rolling back into town without so much as a howdy-do.

"Why the hell did you even come back here, Katy?" he demanded the minute she was close enough to hear. "Was it so you could twist the knife still lodged between his ribs just a little bit deeper? Did you want to see him bleed for you in person?"

Katy stared at him aghast and wide-eyed, reeling at the fury in his tone if not in his words.

"Well, congratulations, Miss High-and-Mighty Wallace, you've accomplished all that and more."

She immediately opened her mouth to protest, but Ethan's upraised hand and the negative shake of his head quickly cut off what would have been her insistent denial.

"No, don't say anything, Katy. I don't want to hear your excuses right now and I don't think I could stomach the lies. I do want you to do me a favor, though, and it's one I think even you can handle just fine. When you leave tomorrow? This time when you go?"

He stopped, shaking his head as if the fury he felt was making the words he meant to say get stuck somewhere between his mouth and his mind. "This time when you leave, Katy, once you're sure you're through twisting the hilt of the knife? You make damned good and sure you stay gone."

CHAPTER 17

Katy almost stayed locked in her room at her mothers instead of joining her friends at what would be her last Saturday night Rumor Creek bonfire. The afternoon weather report had mentioned another dip into cold for the evening and although she'd gotten a bit used to much colder winters up north, she knew the after dark chill would still make the night uncomfortable —both from the weather and at least one of her friends.

If it weren't for the nagging voice in her head that said she only wanted to skip out because she was too cowardly to face her friends after foisting an outsider on them last night, she would have. Katy Wallace was no coward, even if she did feel very much like a fraud because she'd told no one of her decision to break her engagement to Tipton—including Tipton himself.

Every minute she had to sit and smile and nod through good-natured bits of marital advice and congratulations she did not deserve seemed to put one more chink in her "I-can-do-this" armor.

Tonight she would be alone, however. After the mess of unmerciful teasing he'd suffered at the Horseshoe last night, Tipton had elected to stay at the hotel to catch up on some work while Katy went out to Rumor Creek with her friends for one last Saturday night *hoo-rah* in her home town.

He would be leaving tomorrow afternoon; she was going to drive him to the airport, and then she would follow him back up on Monday. Sometime between now and then, she would have to tell him she'd decided to call off the wedding. She just needed to find the right time.

Needing the timing to be perfect reminded her of Matthew and the proposal he hadn't managed to make because she'd left before he'd decided the moment was right—and they'd lost each other and what might have been because of it. She didn't want to waste any more of her life by taking too long to break her engagement to Tipton and that realization urged her into action. Shrugging into her coat while carefully skirting the fire, she almost ran into Ethan in her hurry to get back to her car. He hadn't spoken to her all night but she had felt the fiery blast of his glare from all the way across the bonfire.

"I'm not going to marry him, Ethan," she blurted

when he reached out and caught her by the shoulders to save her from a collision.

He scoffed. "Tell me something I don't know."

"I'm not talking about Matthew," she corrected. "I am talking about my *fiancé*, Tipton. I'm calling off the wedding."

Ethan processed the news in stoic silence though the look in his eyes said he was skeptical. "Well, this is interesting news. What changed your mind? Have you told anyone else?"

She shook her head. "No, I haven't. As a matter of fact, I haven't even told my *fiancé* yet, and I kind of think he's the one who really ought to know, don't you?"

Katy colored with the heat of a blush, and gave a sheepish sort of shrug. "I'm a bit of a coward, I suppose, but I'm planning to tell him tonight when I get home. That's where I was headed, by the way; why I'm heading out early from the bonfire tonight—Tipton's leaving tomorrow."

Ethan looked uncomfortable, something for him that was totally uncharacteristic. She could tell by his wary expression he wanted to believe her but at the same time he was equally as unsure trusting her again would be a safe thing for him to do.

"Don't worry, it's as good as a fact, Ethan, but please don't say anything to the others." Especially Matthew, she wanted to add, but kept that name in particular to herself. "I really think Tipton should be the first to know—well, the second considering I've just told you. But after last night, I thought I should—no, don't apologize."

She knew he was about to ask her forgiveness for having chewed her out last night, so she stopped him with a quick reassurance that she'd understood exactly where he'd been coming from.

"I know you were angry with me, Ethan. I know that underneath that neutral exterior somewhere you still are. I get it, I promise. You know I do, and you shouldn't worry. I don't blame you at all."

The imploring look she gave him begged understanding. "But about Tipton and the engagement thing? I just wanted you to know."

"So you're staying here, then? Staying home in Vine Falls?" His gaze slid to Matthew, and she shook her head.

Katy lowered her gaze for a minute before she lifted her chin to answer. "No. I'm still leaving, Ethan. My flight doesn't leave until Monday, but don't worry—once I'm gone from here this time, I'm not coming back."

With all the memories forever locked in this place for her, memories her heart simply could not bear, Katy didn't think she'd ever be able to come back for the rest of her life.

"Katy, I didn't mean—" he started but she cut him off.

"No, I told you I get it, Ethan. I know what you

meant and I know why you said what you said. If I were in your place, I probably would have told me off, too," she said, giving him a wry, somewhat smirkish grin.

Ethan grinned back. "Yeah, you would, only I'll bet your choice of words would have been a lot more colorful, and there might have been some fingernails and hissing involved. You always have been kind of a hellcat over Matthew."

Katy tried to smile but emotion was making her lips warp and twist in ways that didn't look cheery at all. Ethan behaved as a true gentleman would by pretending not to notice.

"I didn't mean it when I said you should never come back, Katy," he said after a minute, giving a wry grin of his own. "You are my friend, you know, and I'd miss the hell out of you—we've all missed you since you've been gone. But we've all had to live with our good old buddy, Matthew. Day after day after day."

He tried to inject a bit of teasing into his words, but Katy heard them in the serious tone she knew he'd actually meant them. Matthew was his friend, too, and Ethan probably knew best just how badly she'd hurt him. Looking back, Katy almost wished she could start over, wished she could come home and do it all again, only differently but it was just to late for that.

Last night Matthew had said goodbye. She had seen it in his eyes in that minute before he'd left the Horseshoe. The look he had given her said was over her now and for him there would be no going back. Swallowing back unbidden tears, she said, "I never meant to hurt him, Ethan. At least not as much as I seem to have done by leaving four years ago. We were young. I thought he would forget, that in time he would get over it. Over me...."

"You mean like you got over him?" Ethan asked, giving her a pointed look. He could have meant it a number of ways but tonight all Katy heard was sharp accusation, that she didn't care one bit about Matthew when God knew the exact opposite was true. Tonight, his words were like a dagger plunging into her already battered and broken heart, and she drew up, her gaze whipping back into a fiery lock with his.

"Yes, just like that, Ethan. *Exactly* like that," she snapped a bit waspishly, nodding her head as she re-situated the strap of her purse on her shoulder. "But I promise he'll stop hurting now."

Unlike herself, she thought as she walked away, climbing the hill back up to her car. It seemed *she* was destined to go on hurting forever.

Buckling her seat belt into place, she glanced into her rear view mirror for one last look at what once had been part of the happiest years of her life. The fire was still blazing, the music was still loud—she could hear it here in her car. Behind her, her friends continued to dance, to laugh, to enjoy themselves the same as they had always done while she looked on from a distance in the frigid interior of her car.

It was a typical Saturday night throw-down on Rumor Creek. Second only to the night she'd taken the bus out of here four years ago, it was the saddest, loneliest, most miserably heartbreaking night of her life.

Katy switched on the engine and carefully maneuvered her own vehicle out around the other cars but she didn't go back to her mother's. Instead, she drove straight to the hotel where Tipton was staying and took the elevator up to his room.

He opened the door to her insistent knock wearing nothing but a pair of flannel pajama bottoms and she realized this was the most she had seen of his body during the entire eight months of their engagement.

"What are you doing here, Katy? It's late and you smell like a forest fire. Do you know it is practically the middle of the night?"

It wasn't. It was barely after ten, but she didn't bother to correct him. Averting her gaze from the unexpected display of his surprisingly well-defined bare chest which left her feeling strangely unaffected considering this man had been, until a few days ago, the man she intended to marry, she pushed past him and didn't stop until she was standing in the center of the room. There, she pivoted and turned, locking her gaze with his as she got straight to the point of her purportedly late-night visit.

"This couldn't wait, I'm afraid. Tipton, we have to talk—about something I think you might actually find important." Steeling herself for his reaction, whatever it might be, she took a deep breath and just blurted out what she had come here to say. "I'm calling off the wedding."

For a long moment of silence he only stared at her but she could see the thoughts in his mind ticking like the hands of a dusty clock. Finally, his eyes narrowed a bit. "This is about that guy in the bar last night, isn't it?"

Katy wanted to say yes because it was partly true, but Matthew wasn't all of it. "No, actually Tipton, this is about me and you and our relationship. You might find it a bit surprising to know, but there is something definitely missing."

That seemed to break whatever musing trance he'd fallen into. His lips quirked up on one side in a bemused smile. "Please. You cannot possibly be serious, Katy. We aren't even married yet and I've already given you everything a woman could possibly want."

Cocking her head to the side she peered at him. "And what do we want, Tipton, in your estimation? Is it status? Diamonds? Media classes and a brand new wardrobe to match the brand new car?"

"I didn't give you the car," he pointed out and she scoffed.

"And I don't think that's what is missing from our relationship. I am talking about *love*, Tipton, that deep-down emotion that comes from your heart and makes you do crazy things?"

"You think I don't love you? Is that why you're here? But Katy, you know that I do. I love that you're smart and stylish and you're always on time." He tilted his head and smiled, holding out both hands to her in supplication, but she only stared at him until he let them fall to his sides again. "Alright, Katy. What is it you want me to do?"

"I don't want you to do anything, Tipton," she said, feeling wilted and weary, but also strangely calm and light. "This isn't about you anymore. It's about me and what I want in life and I've realized that status and diamonds and a man who cares more about how we look on camera or to his friends than how I feel isn't it."

He arched a brow. "And the guy at the bar, he knows what you want?"

"Yes! But that's not the only thing, Tipton. Matthew not only knows what I want, he also cares about how I feel. Me. My feelings, my happiness is important to him. Can you honestly say the same?"

His brow furrowed. "I never wished for you to be unhappy, Katy. I thought you were happy to be with me."

"I *was*. I am. But only as a friend. From a husband, though, I want *more* and I'm afraid what I want is really more than you can give." Sliding the ring from her finger, she held it out to him. "I'm sorry, but I can't marry you, Tipton."

CHAPTER 18

When Katy's alarm went off for a second time late the next morning—or had it gone afternoon already?—it felt like she'd barely closed her eyes to sleep. After driving Tipton to the airport, she'd rushed straight home with one thing on her mind: call Matthew and beg him to meet her someplace where they could talk—but it was too early, and then she'd spent too many hours imagining scenarios of how their conversation might go.

She didn't remember falling asleep, but the next thing she knew her alarm was blaring again. Before she even had time to roll groggily out of bed and fumble through putting her clothes on, her phone rang. Glaring at the thing and grumbling a string of not nice words beneath her breath about rotten timing, she picked it up, swiped the screen and brought the phone to her ear, sleepily mumbling a gravelly, "Hello?"

"I know it's barely after eleven but don't you dare go anywhere," LoraLynn said, her cheery voice erupting in her ear as soon as Katy answered. "I need a lift to the church; it's important and everyone else is busy. BobbyJoe has my car."

Tired and grumpy from not enough sleep and too many mismatched thoughts running around in her head, Katy tried to put her off. The last thing she wanted to do this afternoon was get up and get dressed then drive down to take LoraLynn to the church reception hall. On a Sunday.

They'd arrive just as services were letting out and she knew how bad that would look, but LoraLynn insisted, keeping on until Katy finally gave in, though she refused to say exactly why she specifically needed *her* to be there. She'd also sworn dropping her off wouldn't work either.

"Oh, no, you have to come with me. Come on, Katy, it won't take long," she insisted, which was why, forty-five minutes later, Katy was sitting in the church parking lot with LoraLynn, trying to argue her way out of going inside.

"Would you just get out?" LoraLynn demanded, finally showing signs of being exasperated, and although she did so grudgingly with lots of grumbling going on under her breath, Katy gave in yet again.

"I really should be packing," Katy tried again at the steps, but LoraLynn just shook her head and rushed to get ahead of her.

"Wait. Hold on," she said at the door and cracked it open a bit before leaning close to peer inside. "Are we ready?" she hissed in a stage whisper that had Katy rolling her eyes though she had to admit the hint of secrecy now had her curiosity piqued.

"Yes? Okay Katy, now we can go inside." Pushing the double doors open wide, she stepped to one side while urging Katy forward.

There were balloons—everywhere.

The tables were all draped in white and there were several bouquets of fresh flowers.

One table at the back was covered with stacks of gaily wrapped gifts and the others were spread with little cakes and a stunning array of suddenly appetizing finger foods. When was the last time she'd eaten, anyway?

Before she could figure it out, a shower of rose petals appeared out of nowhere, drenching her in their sweet aroma as the smiling faces of a number of ladies—as many of her old acquaintances and friends as she could easily put a name to—popped into view and Katy found herself bombarded.

"Surprise!"

Eyes wide, she turned to stare in horror at LoraLynn. "What exactly are we doing here, LoraLynn?" she asked, her voice holding an edge of bafflement and unease. "What in the world is going on?"

LoraLynn laughed and gave her a hug before patting her on the shoulder. "I forgot you've never done this before. This is a going away bridal shower."

Bridal shower? *Oh, no.* Shaking her head in a rapid signal for no, she said, "LoraLynn, wait. We can't do this. Y'all shouldn't have, I—"

Closing her eyes, she started again, putting her hands up in front of her. "There's something I really need to—"

"Let's start with the presents," Sadie said, her voice as filled with excitement as a two year old on the holidays. Bouncing up beside Katy, she held out a present—it was wrapped in shining paper, red, with a big gold bow. "This one's from me, of course. I want you to open it first."

The next thing Katy knew, she was sitting in a chair in the center of the room with a pile of presents and mounds of torn gift wrap surrounding her. Most of the others congratulated her on her upcoming wedding and slipped away after that, leaving Katy with a few of her closest friends and a whole lot of household gadgets she might never get a chance to use.

"Look, y'all. She's speechless!" Amber laughed. "Never thought there would come a day when Katy had nothing to say."

Taking a deep breath, Katy lifted her chin and

looked them all in the eye, one by one. "I can't keep them. I'm not getting married."

"We know the wedding's not until July, but—wait, what did you say?" Sadie asked, blinking in confusion.

Taking another deep breath and releasing it on a quick sigh, Katy repeated what she'd said, only this time she added a few words of explanation to be sure no one could misunderstand. "I said *I'm not getting married*. I called off the wedding last night. I drove to the hotel when I left the bonfire to break the news to Tipton. We aren't getting married anymore. He went home alone. He flew out this morning."

LoraLynn gave her a speculative look and walked over to another table where she picked up another rectangular package from behind a punch bowl still swimming with foamy green punch.

"I guess it's a good thing I saved this one for last, then. He asked me to wait until everyone else had gone before I gave it to you." She shrugged. "Everyone else is gone, besides us, so I guess now is okay."

Katy started to protest but then she felt everything inside her pause when LoraLynn handed over that one last gift. The card on top said it was a gift from Matthew and a terrible feeling bloomed in her chest; it felt something like sadness only ten times worse and Katy had a moment where she actually thought she might do something crazy, like sit in the middle of the floor with the gift in her lap and just cry.

The present from Matthew was colorfully wrapped like all the others, in a shirt box, no less. But when Katy opened it to find an official-looking envelope inside, her brow furrowed in curious surprise. With shaking fingers, which she slid beneath the flap, she opened the envelope and carefully removed the contents—a stack of documents that turned out to be a deed to the property running along both sides of Rumor Creek—and it had her name on it.

Her throat seized up as all her emotions rose to the fore and threatened to overwhelm her. Everything meaningful that had ever happened in her life had happened at Rumor Creek and now Matthew had just handed it over to her with no strings attached; it was as if he had given her the moon. Feeling as if her heart had been ripped from her chest and then handed to her, shredded and bleeding in ribbons and bows, she turned tear-filled eyes first to Amber and then LoraLynn. Her voice thick and hoarse with tears, she asked, "What am I supposed to do now?"

"You know, Katy, you probably think you've been hiding your emotions from us pretty well but we're not blind, sweetie. Sadie, Amber, Gin and Erin and I, we all have eyes and we can plainly see what's been going on between you and Matthew." Laying her hand consolingly against Katy's shoulder, LoraLynn asked, "You still love him, don't you?"

If her flush hadn't given her away, the second rush of tears hurriedly covered by a quick nod surely did, but ...

"I can't," she began but had to stop to gather her composure. She tried again. "It's a wonderful gift. It's more than I ever could have hoped for, actually," she said with a watery laugh. "But I can't keep it. It doesn't change anything and I can't let it matter. I promised Ethan I wouldn't hurt him again and if I keep this—"

"Why are you tearing him all up inside again like you did four years ago?" LoraLynn demanded in a friendly yet serious manner. "Look, I'm your friend, and I love you, girl, but we all think Matthew has been hurt enough. He is our friend, too, you know."

Putting a hand on Katy's shoulder, she gave her an encouraging little pat and said, "*Tell* him."

Katy wished it were as simple as that. "Matthew doesn't care anymore, LoraLynn. He told me so last night. Not in so many words, but it was plain enough to understand if you read between the lines. And you don't know what I've said or the things I've done. Well, you know some of them, but Matthew—" she paused, drawing in a quick, jerky breath. "Matthew doesn't love me anymore, and hey, who here can blame him, right? Certainly not me."

Tearing up yet again, her brow furrowed as she shook

her head and sighed. "If he did, he would have said something, LoraLynn—if not when I first got here then when Tipton showed up, for sure."

"Matthew doesn't love you? Matthew Shaw doesn't care?" LoraLynn laughed, genuine surprise mixing with the utter disbelief in her tone. "Are you sure we are talking about the same person here?"

"Well who else would we be talking about?" Katy drawled.

Ignoring her sarcastic quip, LoraLynn continued. "You know who carried you to your room the other night, Katy, when you were a little too blitzed to walk up the stairs by yourself? It was Matthew, and as we were about to leave, he leaned over to tuck your hair back and said..."

She swallowed, then laughed; her voice had gone taut and seemed a bit strained. With one finger, she wiped at the corner of her eye and sniffed. "It's amazing how emotional a body gets over the love of someone else isn't it?"

"What? What did he say?" Katy pressed, waiting on tenterhooks, feeling like everything important in her life hung in the balance with whatever LoraLynn was about to reveal.

LoraLynn's throat worked for a second and she ducked her head, closing her eyes presumably to keep her tears at bay. Finally, she lifted her head. "He said *I'll always love you, fairy girl.*"

Shaking her head in a gesture of inexplicable awe, she said, "I swear that almost killed me, Katy, hearing him tell you that. You were out of it so of course you couldn't hear what I heard or know what I saw, but there was such pain mixed with the hunger I know I saw in his eyes and so much wistful longing in his voice..."

"Oh, y'all have got to stop this," Amber piped up suddenly. "Otherwise we'll all be sitting here with our heads in our hands, bawling and wiping away tears. And did y'all forget we're in the reception hall at the church? We can't even have wine with all this cheese!"

Sadie laughed, not even bothering to try and hide that she was already swiping at tears. "It is beautiful, though, isn't it, Amber? How many of us can say we've experienced something as equally tragic and wonderfully romantic as this love/hate thing going on between Matthew and Katy?"

"I've never hated Matthew," Katy hastened to correct. "Never."

Sadie laughed again. "My point exactly. You've *never* hated him. He's never hated *you*. Don't you think four years is long enough for either of you to love someone and still remain apart?"

"Didn't BobbyJoe mention something about Matthew dropping by the auto parts place to pick up something for Ethan this afternoon?" Amber gave Katy a marked look and pointed toward the window. "It's three blocks *that* way. Why don't you go over and have a little chat with him? We'll all wait right here."

"Actually, he drove to Atlanta to pick up that part Ethan needed for his tractor, Amber," Sadie interjected, her lips drawn in a tiny frown. She glanced at Katy, her expression apologetic. "Jensen said he saw him go by right before I left to come over here. Nobody's gonna be seeing him for a good six hours or so, and that's assuming he doesn't have to wait on the delivery guy when he gets there."

"But we definitely know he's going to head straight to Ethan's when he comes back, right?" Erin shrugged. "You could always drive over and meet him there."

Katy's stomach did a sickly miserable little flip-flop and her hand slid downward to rest against her middle as if to hold it in place. She wouldn't meet him at Ethan's. More like she couldn't. But her insides were already giving her fits from just thinking she might drum up enough courage after everything that had been said and done to drive out and meet him anywhere.

Even if she couldn't say anything else, this time she knew she needed to at least say goodbye.

Six hours was going to feel like forever.

CHAPTER 19

The sun had already started to go down when Matthew pulled up and parked in the driveway beside Ethan's burnt orange colored Dodge pickup truck. He honked the horn to let Ethan know he'd arrived. The sound of the front screen door banging shut said Ethan was on his way and Matthew got out of his own truck, hitching up the back of his jeans as he went around to the back. complaining all the while.

"Had to wait *again*, Jones. Three hours this time. It's a good thing Waffle House never runs out of coffee. I seriously think your boys up there need to look into getting a new parts pick-up guy." He jumped up on the back bumper. Leaning over the tailgate to heft the boxed part Ethan had asked him to pick up from of the bed of his truck, Matthew grunted as he passed it over.

"Thanks, man. I would've never managed to get the combine out there to the back field in the morning without this." Ethan hefted the part onto his shoulder and then walked over to load it into the back of his pickup, but rather than saying goodbye and going back up to the house, he turned around and leaned against the bumper, pinning Matthew with a look that said he might as well stick around a while.

"I hear Katy's flying out tomorrow. Headed north again with that fellow who showed up with her over at the Horseshoe the other night."

"You mean her *fiancé*?" Matthew gritted, hiding his tension behind a falsely nonchalant shrug. "Figured they'd be heading out soon enough."

Ethan's narrow-eyed stare said he'd picked up on something revealing in Matthew's tone but he wasn't going to mention it. Yet. "Why don't you ask her to stay this time? The past couple weeks have almost been like the good ol' days, only we weren't counting down the days to prom or graduation."

"Except for Katy, who's been counting down days to a wedding." A reminiscent smile ghosted Matthew's lips before he let his gaze drop to the ground where he scuffed at the ground with his boots. "Yeah, it has been fun, hasn't it? But you know Katy. Here one minute, gone the next. Off without a moment's notice."

If anyone could have guessed at the depths of true

pain hidden behind that comment, it would have to be Ethan. He peered at Matthew, one eyebrow slightly arched. "Katy's not that girl anymore, Matthew. Ask her. I think she'll stay."

As much as he wished what Ethan had said was true, Matthew knew it wasn't. He shook his head.

"I heard the girls all got together today to give her a shower, or whatever those pre-wedding things are called. And come on, Ethan. You've talked to her since she's been back, so you know Katy wants the same thing now that she wanted four years ago. *Escape.* A way out."

"I talked to her. I also saw her the night after you gave her the ring. You know what? She bawled like a baby, Matthew." Peering pointedly over at him, Ethan asked, "How many times between us do you reckon we've ever seeing Katy cry?"

"Once or twice." He shrugged, then frowned. "Not many, I guess, but that's beside the point. She told me herself she doesn't want to be trapped here—she doesn't want to be like the rest of us; just another small town statistic."

Unconsciously, Matthew used the exact same words Katy had used to describe her feelings when she'd left him practically standing at the altar four years ago. "That's why she left the first time, you know."

Ethan cocked his head to the side and Matthew recognized the determined, mulish look in his eye long before he said, "I didn't, actually, and I'm not so sure about that. Maybe she *did* think it, or maybe she only thought it way back when, but what if that's *not* what she thinks anymore? What if *this* time she's actually hoping for a reason to stay?"

A reason to stay? Ethan couldn't possibly know how deeply those words cut but Matthew knew he was bleeding. If his love hadn't been reason enough for Katy to stay four years ago, it wasn't going to be enough now, nor would it ever be. Not to mention Katy was currently very much engaged.

Feeling as if he'd aged ten years in the past three weeks, Matthew snorted.

"Even if she is, Ethan, I won't be the one to offer it." He'd already given her everything he had to give. Shoving his hands deep into the pockets of his jeans, he said, "I'm never going to change, Ethan. I am what I am. As far as Katy is concerned, I'll always be the same old same old, which means not enough, and she deserves more than that. A lot more."

"Well if you ask me, a good, hard-working man who loves her more than just about anything life has to offer is plenty enough, and way more than most ever get." Ethan stood, pushing away from the back of the truck bed and shook his head. "Any woman could do worse than hook up with Matthew Shaw. A helluva lot worse."

"Yeah, now there's something I can definitely agree

with, for sure." Matthew nodded at that and grinned. "See, I think it'd be a heck of a lot worse for a woman to end up with you!"

Ethan snorted and held up a hand indicating he was done with this conversation. "Whatever. Thanks for picking up the part, man. I'll see you Friday, I guess?"

Matthew shrugged a non-answer answer and he didn't stand around after that, but something made Ethan hold back even after the taillights on Matthew's truck disappeared in the dust. He stood there waiting by the truck, one booted foot propped against the back bumper again until, a short while later, he finally saw something that made him smile.

Glancing down at his watch he smirked and gave his head a shake while his shoulders shook with silent laughter. Katy. He should have known.

He waited until she slowed the car to a halt and let down the passenger side window. "Well, look at that, won't ya? Matthew hasn't been gone a full ten minutes and here *you* come, high-tailing it up the drive. Reminds me of another time at the same place with the same old high school kids. What's up, Katy? Let me guess ... you're looking for Matthew so you two can sneak down to old man Peterman's place and lark it up again?"

Katy's head dropped back against the headrest of the driver's seat and she groaned. "I missed him? Really?"

Ethan grunted and walked over to lean into the car

through the window so he could hear her better. "So I'm right. You were trying to catch him. What I suddenly find myself curious to know, though, after our chat at the bonfire last night is in the ever lovin' hell why?"

She hadn't killed the engine so the dashboard lights did a fair job of revealing her worn features that seemed far too fragile; she was way too close to bursting into tears at the moment for his comfort. "Come on, Ethan. I promised you I wouldn't hurt him anymore but I think we both can agree that this time he at least deserves a proper goodbye."

Ethan mulled that over in his head for a minute, then glanced back over his shoulder toward the road. "I'm surprised you didn't pass him back there. I guess he decided not to go straight home."

"Guess not, because I didn't see him." Her brow furrowed and she sighed. "Any idea where he might have gone?"

Ethan's expression was one of mocking. "Come on, Katy. I think we can both agree that from here there's only one other road he might have taken—and I'm pretty sure you remember exactly where it leads. Am I right?"

She did know. She nodded. "He's gone to Rumor Creek."

Putting the vehicle in reverse, she offered a weary but sincere smile. "Thanks, Ethan. And don't worry about Matthew. I'm only going to say goodbye—I promise."

Thumping his open palm against the door panel, Ethan pushed back out of the window. "You do that, Katy. Oh, and since I won't be around when you leave to tell you, have a nice flight out tomorrow."

As he watched her back out of the drive, her words playing in his head, he knew she meant what she'd said: she was going to say goodbye to Matthew to try and make up for not having done so last time. What he'd like to be there to know, though, once she had her say, was whether or not Matthew would still be foolish enough to actually let her leave.

⋆

SOMEHOW, Katy knew the exact spot she would find him: he would be at *their* place. The spot where they had shared a picnic together just a few days ago. As she flipped on her turn signal and followed the road to the right, she had no doubt she would find Matthew wandering in the dark in the clearing where they'd spent one perfect night together for her first time, beneath a circle of tall water oaks on the eastern-most side of Rumor Creek.

Knowing he had a good fifteen minute lead on her, she hurried every chance she got—she didn't want to miss him again. This was the last chance she had of seeing him before she left in the morning and she desperately needed to talk to him—about her broken engagement to Tipton. The ring. About so many things. But recalling the look he'd given her the last time she'd seen him, she suddenly worried if he would even be willing to listen.

To try and calm her sudden onset of jangled nerves, Katy reached over and pressed play on the CD she had left in the drive, flooding the car with memory as well as melody. It didn't help, so she punched the button one more time to shut the thing back off.

And then she was there in the stretch of rocky dirt that was the only safe place available to park, and she quickly did so, in a hurry now to kill the engine. She didn't want Matthew to hear the car, but at the same time, she felt a little hesitant about trying to surprise him. She might still be a country girl at heart, but the thought of running across a rattler in the dark still had the power to terrify her.

Sliding her arms into the long sleeves of her hoodie, Katy stepped out of the car and walked around the back, her eyes squinting against the darkness as she tried to pick out the faint trail that would lead her down the hill to the clearing where she expected Matthew to be.

She was wrong about where she would find him, she soon discovered. She hadn't taken two steps from the car when his voice came out of the darkness, and he sounded a lot closer than she thought he would be.

"It's dark, and you shouldn't be out driving alone," he said, and she jumped. One hand flew up to her chest, the other to her mouth to quickly squelch the scream of fright that had risen unbidden to her lips. Spinning about, she scanned the night, willing her eyes to adjust. Finally, she managed to locate him—he was sitting with his back against the cab in the back of his truck, alone in the dark with his thoughts.

"My stars, Matthew!" she finally breathed. "You almost frightened the life right out of me!"

Shadows moved and changed in the back of his pickup, looming eerily for a moment until he put both hands on the side and vaulted himself over in one fluid motion, coming to land about two feet in front of her.

"It's late. Don't you have an early plane to catch?" he asked, and then, "What are you doing here, Katy?"

Standing in front of him with barely more than a foot of space between them, Katy lifted her chin, peered up at him, and said, "I came to say goodbye, Matthew. I—I wanted to do it properly this time, and—and I wanted to thank you. For the gift."

After a long moment of tense silence, he nodded. "Fair enough. You've said it. You've thanked me. It's done. Now why don't you do us both a favor? Get back in your car and leave."

Matthew said nothing more, just continued to watch her as she stood there staring back up at him until she took a daring step forward, approaching him cautiously, the way one would a wounded animal.

Reaching out, he caught her by the upper arms, halting all forward movement. His body language said 'keep away' but the soulful look in his eyes said his walls were slowly crumbling and she meant to be there when they fell.

"What is it you want from me?" he whispered, his voice filled with aching pain.

"A kiss? Your love?" Katy whispered back without really realizing she'd said the words out loud until she heard Matthew scoff.

"You've had both and they obviously weren't enough." Releasing her, he held out both hands in front of him, then placed one over his heart. "Loving you has bled me dry. I don't have anything left to give, Katy."

She peered up at him in the dark, her gaze searching. "Does that mean you still have feelings for me?"

He bit back one curse only to grit out another. "Damn it, Katy, you know I do. Do you like seeing me bleed?"

"Ethan seemed to think I do."

Matthew groaned and shook his head right before he let it drop back on his shoulders and closed his eyes. "I swear, woman, as hard to hold and as infuriating as you are, I'll probably go to my grave still loving you."

She stepped closer, her heart pounding. "Oh? Why is that, I wonder?"

He looked back down at her, his gaze direct. "I guess there's just no getting over you."

"But you've tried?" she asked, watching him closely.

"Oh, yes. Lord knows I've tried. For four years I've tried to forget you, Katy, but nothing I've done seems to work," he said as he continued to watch her, his voice soft and yet hard at the same time.

"I was wrong, Matthew," she whispered, her emotions threatening to choke her. "About you. About us. But I didn't realize it until the night you gave me the ring."

His harsh laughter grated and for a second she feared he was going to push her away and demand she leave. But he didn't. "It's a little late for that to matter now, Katy," he said bitterly. "Or did you forget yet again that you're engaged?"

Slowly, Katy shook her head from side to side. "I'm not. Not anymore. I called off the wedding. Tipton flew back yesterday without me."

CHAPTER 20

Matthew stared down at her as everything around him seemed to slow to a grinding halt. Everything but his heart, anyway; that seemed to be pounding double-time. He hardly dared to believe the words she spoke, but neither could he deny the overwhelming swell of emotion they wrought, either.

How many nights since she'd come back had he lain awake hoping the next time he saw her she would tell him she was no longer getting married to some other guy? How many times had he envisioned swooping her up into his arms and kissing the daylights out of her for it?

But now that she'd said what he'd longed to hear he didn't know how to react. Something stilled him, made him proceed with caution. After all, just because she was no longer engaged to someone else didn't mean she was ready to promise herself to him, or even that she wanted to.

Watching her closely, he asked, "You called it off? When?"

"Last night," she answered without hesitation.

Matthew swallowed hard and looked away to gather his thoughts. Finally, he turned back to her. "I don't understand," he said, shaking his head. "Why? After all of this, why? I can't believe you would do such a thing."

"I should think it was obvious why I did it, Matthew," she said.

He shook his head again. "You gotta spell it out for me, Katy."

She stared up at him, her gaze pensive. After a minute, she nodded and looked away. And then she walked away. Matthew wanted to grab her to keep her from leaving again, but it seemed she was only walking to the edge of the clearing. After a moment's hesitation, he followed her.

She turned at the last minute just before he reached her, and said, "Do you have a flashlight in your truck?"

He frowned. "Why?"

She tilted her head in the direction of the trail. "I want to go down that way and I'd rather not run up on a snake."

He hesitated, wondering why she would want to go to their place if she was just going to leave him again.

"Please, Matthew."

It wasn't a question, but it was a plea all the same, and it had the same effect her asking would have. He could never deny her anything, it seemed.

"Wait here," he said, and went to fetch the flashlight he kept in his truck in case of emergencies. He flicked it on when he rejoined her and handed it to her. "Is that better?"

She nodded. "Yes. Thank you."

"You better stomp on your way down. If there are any snakes lurking about, they'll feel the vibrations and know to avoid you."

She nodded again and headed off, her steps heavy and the flashlight's beam steady in front of her, only to stop again when she realized he wasn't following. "You're not coming?" she asked.

He sighed. "Katy..."

"Please? It's important."

Cursing himself for being ten times the fool, he followed.

Soon enough they reached the end of the trail and were standing in the clearing where so many memories had been made and where, on one beautiful summer's morning, Matthew's heart had been ripped from his chest.

The sound of rushing water mingled with the slight breeze and cricket song as Matthew waited for Katy's next move, praying all the while she wouldn't be so cruel as to rip his heart out in the same place twice.

"It's so beautiful here," she said a second later, her voice filled with reverent awe. "I can hardly believe I ever thought I wanted to leave it behind for good."

"Yeah, well, you did," Matthew said, anger and fear and anxiousness making his words come out harsher than he meant for them to. "If all you wanted to come down here for was to reminisce, you can do that on your own. I've got to get back. I've been on the road all day and I'm too tired to fight with you, Katy."

She turned sharply, her eyes wide and scared in the yellow light of the flashlight. "Wait just a little longer, please. Just...please listen to what I have to say."

He stared at her for a long minute, his gaze searching, and then he gave a quiet sigh. "I'm listening."

She nodded and tucked her hair behind her ear. Licking her lips, she took a moment to gather her thoughts, and then she said, "It's been four long years, Matthew, that I've been gone. I've seen and done a lot of things. Certainly more than I ever would have been able to here." She bit her lip and then released it, and her expression grew pensive. "But in all that time, even in my dreams, only one heart called out to me."

"And whose might that be?" Matthew asked softly, waiting on tenterhooks. The look in her eyes turned sharp at the same time her expression softened and she closed the distance between them. He sucked in a breath and held it as she stepped close—so close their bodies touched, and wrapped him in her arms.

Tilting her head back to better see him, she smiled and said, "Yours. There's just no getting over you, either, it seems."

Matthew closed his eyes and groaned harshly an instant before he crushed Katy to him and kissed her until he wasn't sure where he ended and she began. But almost just as quickly he pulled back to look into her eyes and asked, "Does this mean you still love me, Katy?"

Easing away, she reached into the back pocket of her jeans and held up her hand. In the moonlight, he could see the ring he had bought for her so long ago it almost seemed like a dream.

"I've never stopped loving you," she answered. "Not really. But we've wasted so much time." She looked up into his eyes. "Will you marry me, Matthew Shaw? If you say yes, I promise to never leave you again."

He grinned and gave a short bark of laughter just before he wrapped his arms around her and twirled her about. She squealed in surprise and held on tight, laughing breathlessly until, kissing her soundly, Matthew set her back on her feet.

Taking her by the hands, he leaned his head down until their foreheads were touching and said, "Absolutely, fairy girl. You'll never be rid of me."

✳✳✳✳

Get emails for all of Annie Dobbs latest sweet romances:

http://anniedobbs.com/newsletter/

Other Books in the Hometown Harts Series:

A Change of Heart (Book 2)

Join Annie/Leighann's private readers group on Facebook:

https://www.facebook.com/groups/ldobbsreaders/

Would you like a text whenever Annie releases a new romance? Text ROMANCE to 88202 (sorry, this only works for US cell phones!)

ALSO BY ANNIE DOBBS

Sweet Romance (Written As Annie Dobbs)

Hometown Hearts Series

***

No Getting Over You (Book 1)

Magical Romance with a Touch of Mystery

***

Something Magical

Curiously Enchanted

****

Romance and Cozy Mystery - Written as Leighann Dobbs:

Romantic Comedy

***

Corporate Chaos Series

In Over Her Head (book 1)

Can't Stand the Heat (book 2)

Contemporary Romance

***

Reluctant Romance

Cozy Mysteries

Lexy Baker Cozy Mystery Series

* * *

Lexy Baker Cozy Mystery Series Boxed Set Vol 1 (Books 1-4)

Or buy the books separately:

Killer Cupcakes

Dying For Danish

Murder, Money and Marzipan

3 Bodies and a Biscotti

Brownies, Bodies & Bad Guys

Bake, Battle & Roll

Wedded Blintz

Scones, Skulls & Scams

Ice Cream Murder

Mummified Meringues

Brutal Brulee (Novella)

No Scone Unturned

Cream Puff Killer

Mooseamuck Island Cozy Mystery Series

* * *

A Zen For Murder

A Crabby Killer

A Treacherous Treasure

Mystic Notch

Cat Cozy Mystery Series

* * *

Ghostly Paws

A Spirited Tail

A Mew To A Kill

Paws and Effect

Probable Paws

Silver Hollow

Paranormal Cozy Mystery Series

***

A Spell of Trouble (Book 1)

Spell Disaster (Book 2)

Nothing to Croak About (Book 3)

Cry Wolf (Book 4)

Blackmoore Sisters

Cozy Mystery Series

* * *

Dead Wrong

Dead & Buried

Dead Tide

Buried Secrets

Deadly Intentions

A Grave Mistake

Spell Found

Fatal Fortune

Western Historical Romance

***

Goldwater Creek Mail Order Brides:

Faith

American Mail Order Brides Series:

Chevonne: Bride of Oklahoma

ABOUT THE AUTHOR

Annie Dobbs is the pen name of USA Today Bestselling author Leighann Dobbs. Leighann discovered her passion for writing after a twenty year career as a software engineer. She lives in New Hampshire with her husband Bruce, their trusty Chihuahua mix Mojo and beautiful rescue cat, Kitty. When she's not reading, gardening, making jewelry or selling antiques, she likes to write cozy mystery and historical romance books.

Her book "Dead Wrong" won the "Best Mystery Romance" award at the 2014 Indie Romance Convention.

Her book "Ghostly Paws" was the 2015 Chanticleer Mystery & Mayhem First Place category winner in the Animal Mystery category.

Get emails for all of Annie Dobbs latest sweet romances
http://anniedobbs.com/newsletter/

If you want to receive a text message alert on your cell phone for new releases, text ROMANCE to 88202 (sorry, this only works for US cell phones!)

Join Annie/Leighann's private readers group on Facebook:
https://www.facebook.com/groups/ldobbsreaders/

Made in the USA
Middletown, DE
27 July 2023